FERMÍN SOLÍS

ASTRO MOUSE
AND LIGHT BULB

PAPERCUTZ

NEW YORK

FERMÍN SOLÍS

ASTRO MOUSE
AND LIGHT BULB
#1 "Astro Mouse vs. Astro-Chicken"

FERMÍN SOLÍS
Script and Art

© Fermín Solís
© Bang. Ediciones, 2017-2021
contacto@bangediciones.com
All rights reserved.
Originally published as
Astro-Ratón y Bombillita #1: Parece que Chispea, 2008
and *Astro-Ratón y Bombillita #2: Pollo a la vista*, 2012
English translation and all other Editorial Material
© 2021 Papercutz
www.papercutz.com

Paperback ISBN: 978-1-5458-0638-8
Hardcover ISBN: 978-1-5458-0637-1

Special thanks to Stephanie Barrouillet, Agnés Phillippart,
Immaculada Bordell, Léa Jaillard, Maxi Luchini + Ed

Jeff Whitman – Translator, Letterer, Production, Editor
Ingrid Rios – Editorial Assistant
Jim Salicrup
Editor-in-Chief

Printed in China

April 2021

Papercutz books may be purchased for business or
promotional use. For information on bulk purchases
please contact Macmillan Corporate and Premium Sales
Department at (800) 221-7945 x5442.

Distributed by Macmillan

First Papercutz Printing

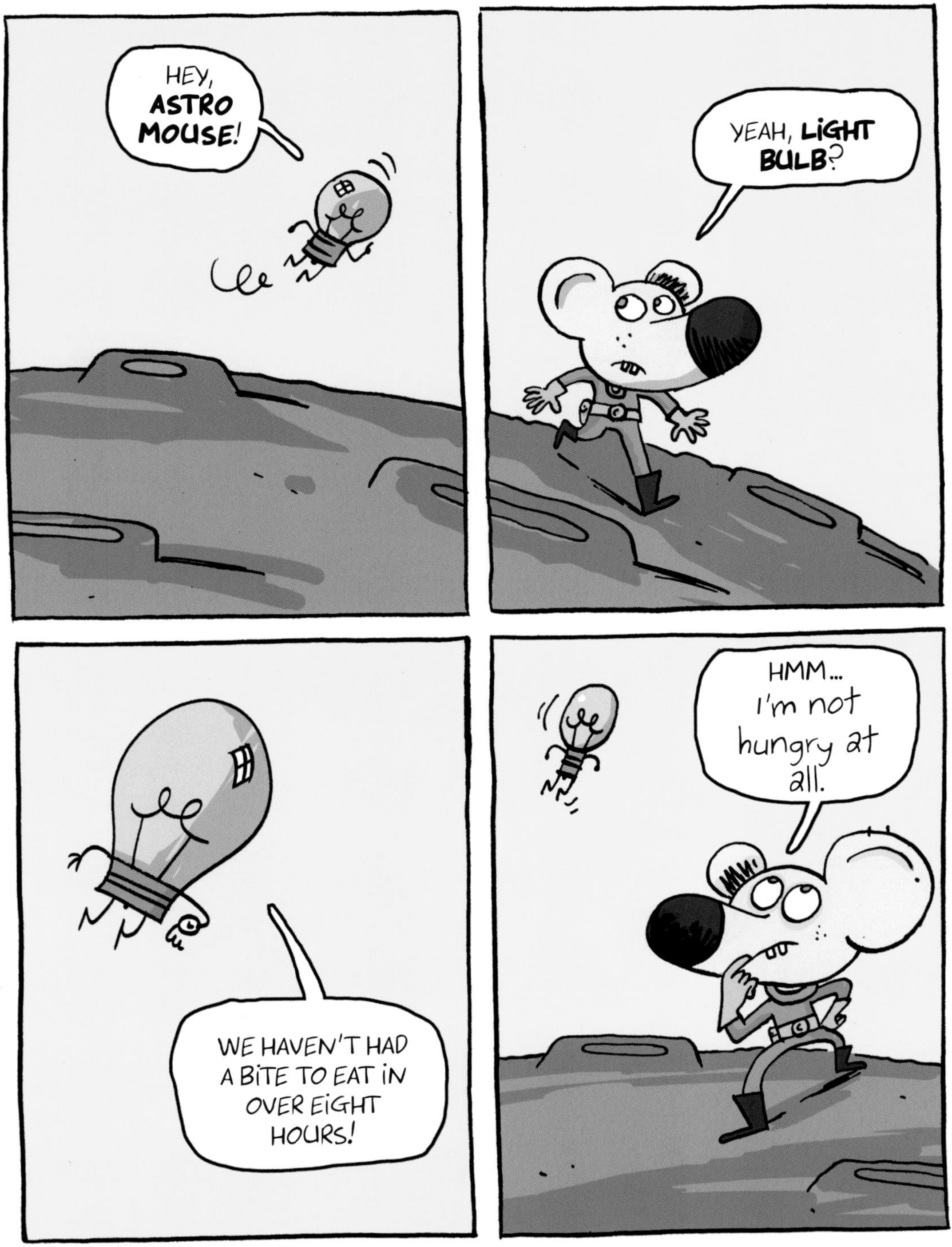

HEY, ASTRO MOUSE!
YEAH, LIGHT BULB?
WE HAVEN'T HAD A BITE TO EAT IN OVER EIGHT HOURS!
HMM... I'm not hungry at all.

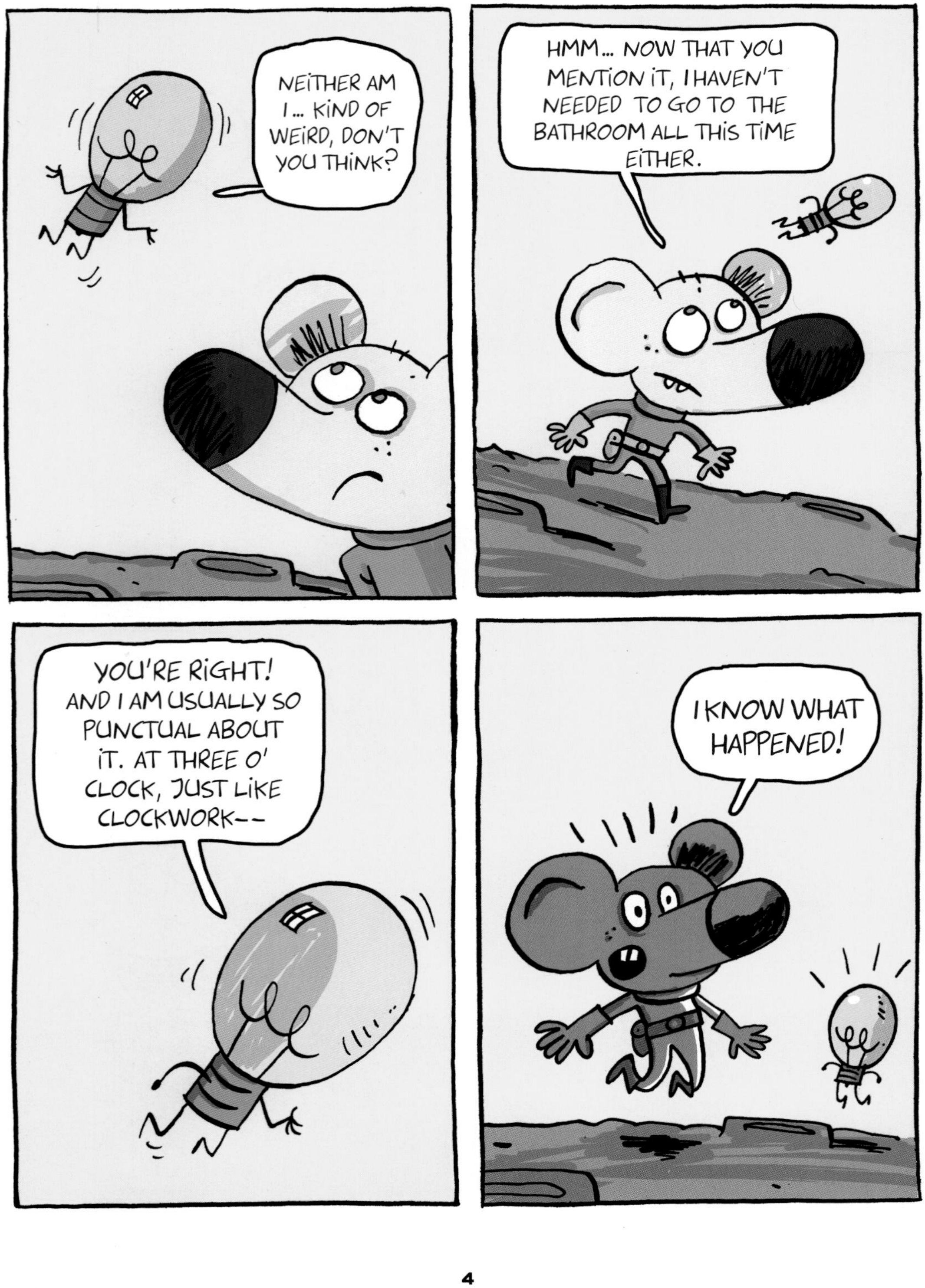
NEITHER AM I... KIND OF WEIRD, DON'T YOU THINK?
HMM... NOW THAT YOU MENTION IT, I HAVEN'T NEEDED TO GO TO THE BATHROOM ALL THIS TIME EITHER.
YOU'RE RIGHT! AND I AM USUALLY SO PUNCTUAL ABOUT IT. AT THREE O' CLOCK, JUST LIKE CLOCKWORK--
I KNOW WHAT HAPPENED!

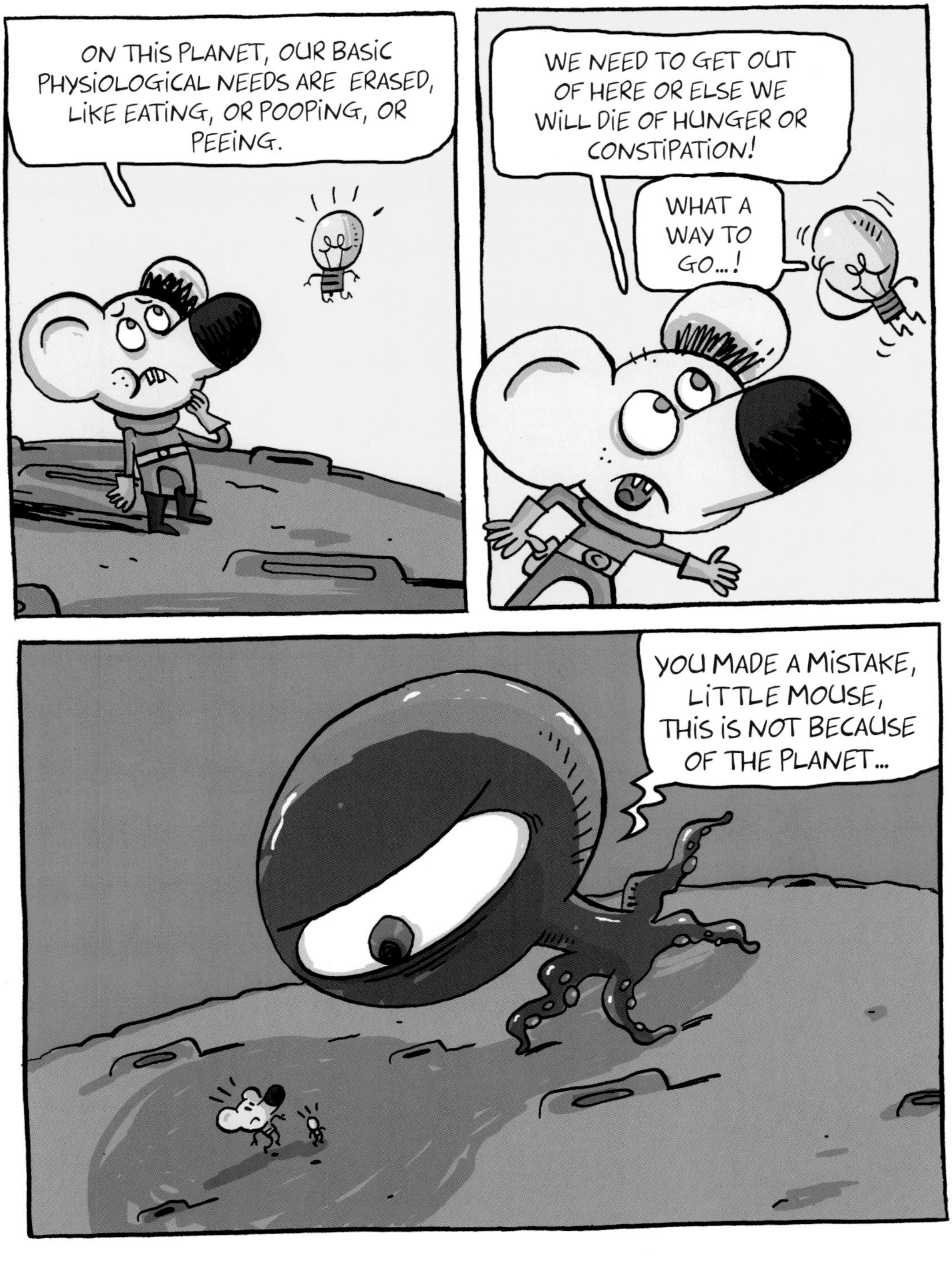
ON THIS PLANET, OUR BASIC PHYSIOLOGICAL NEEDS ARE ERASED, LIKE EATING, OR POOPING, OR PEEING.
WE NEED TO GET OUT OF HERE OR ELSE WE WILL DIE OF HUNGER OR CONSTIPATION!
WHAT A WAY TO GO...!
YOU MADE A MISTAKE, LITTLE MOUSE, THIS IS NOT BECAUSE OF THE PLANET...

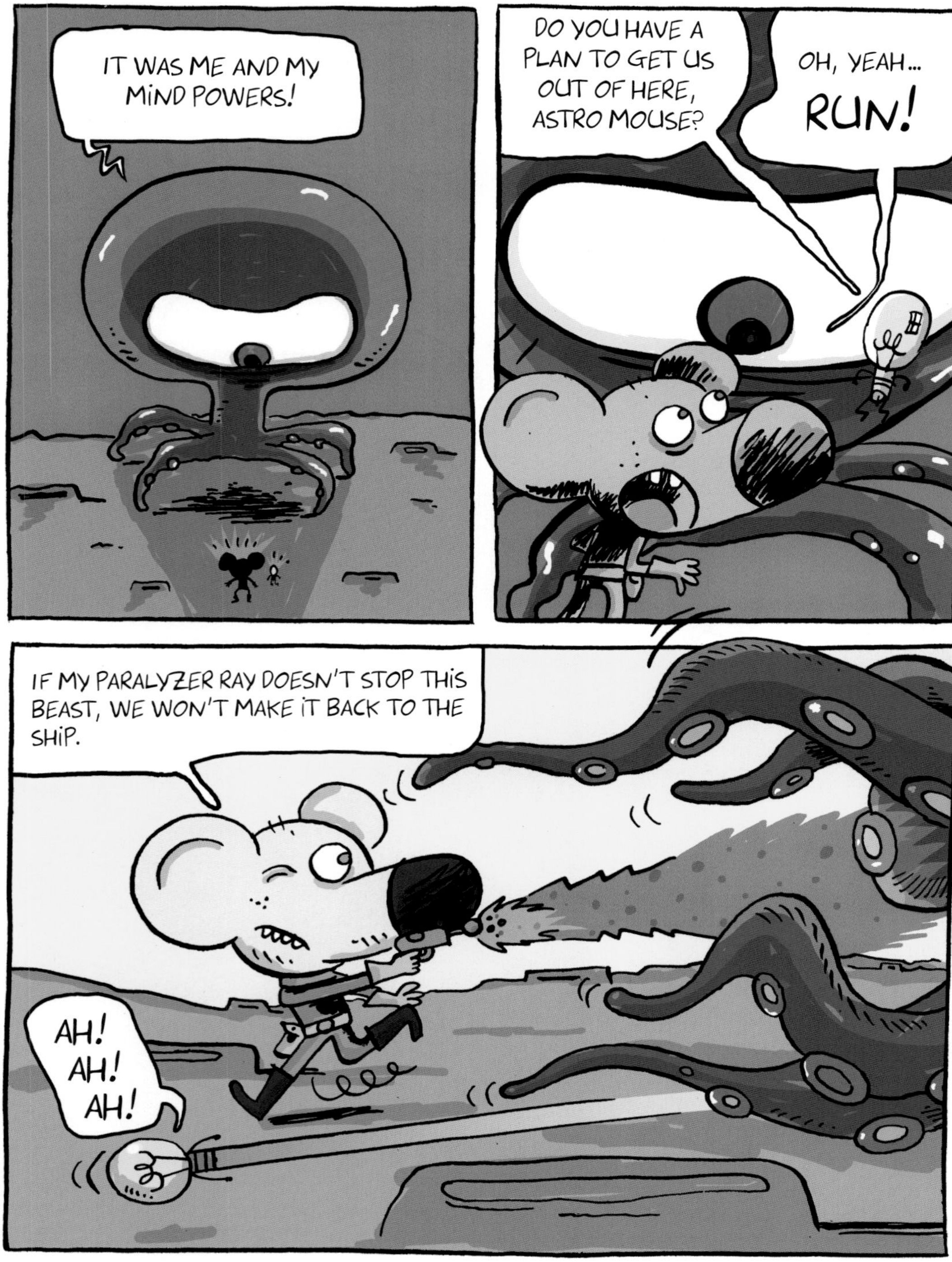
IT WAS ME AND MY MIND POWERS!
DO YOU HAVE A PLAN TO GET US OUT OF HERE, ASTRO MOUSE?
OH, YEAH... RUN!
IF MY PARALYZER RAY DOESN'T STOP THIS BEAST, WE WON'T MAKE IT BACK TO THE SHIP.
AH! AH! AH!

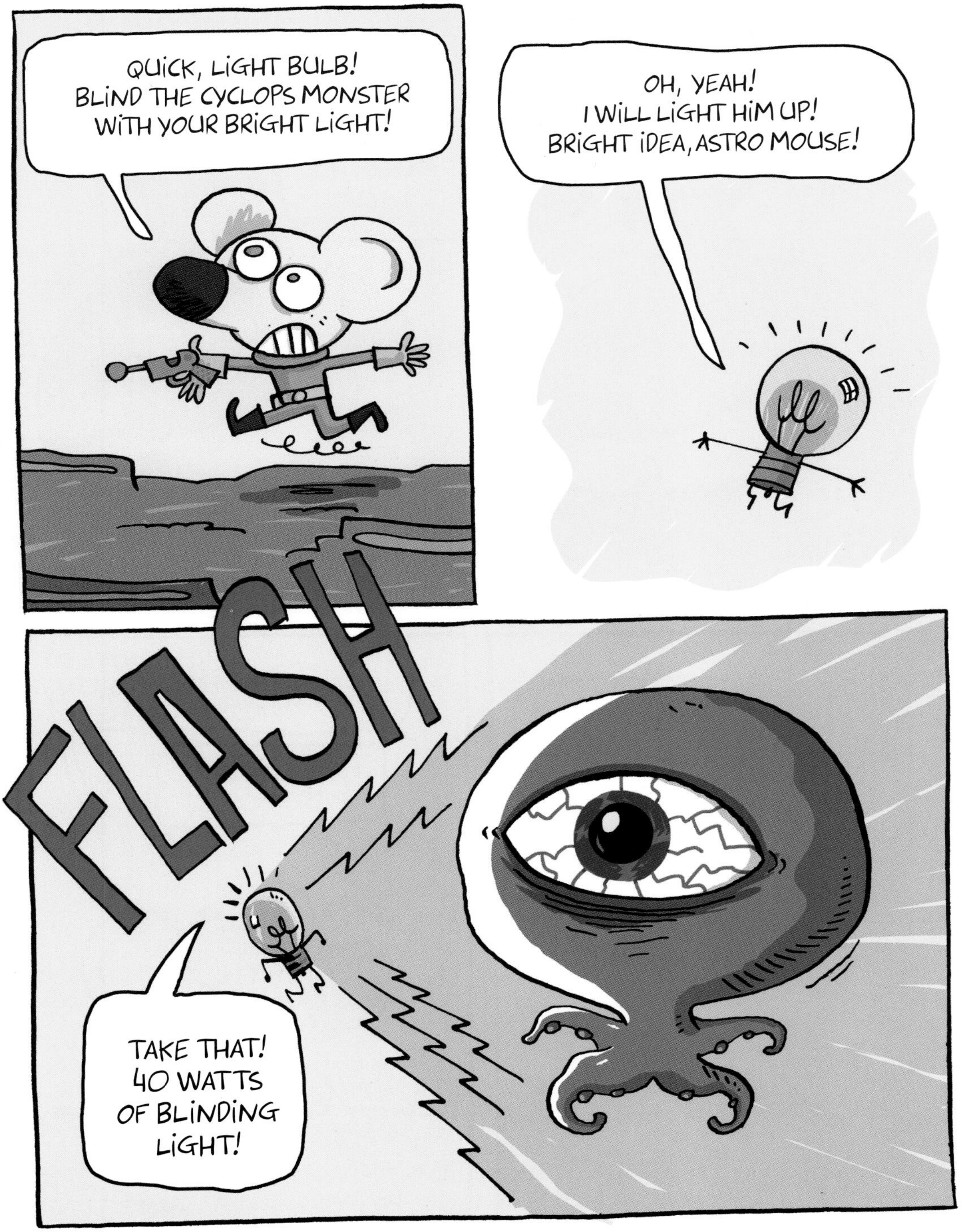
QUICK, LIGHT BULB! BLIND THE CYCLOPS MONSTER WITH YOUR BRIGHT LIGHT!
OH, YEAH! I WILL LIGHT HIM UP! BRIGHT IDEA, ASTRO MOUSE!
FLASH
TAKE THAT! 40 WATTS OF BLINDING LIGHT!

LESS THAN A LIGHT YEAR LATER...

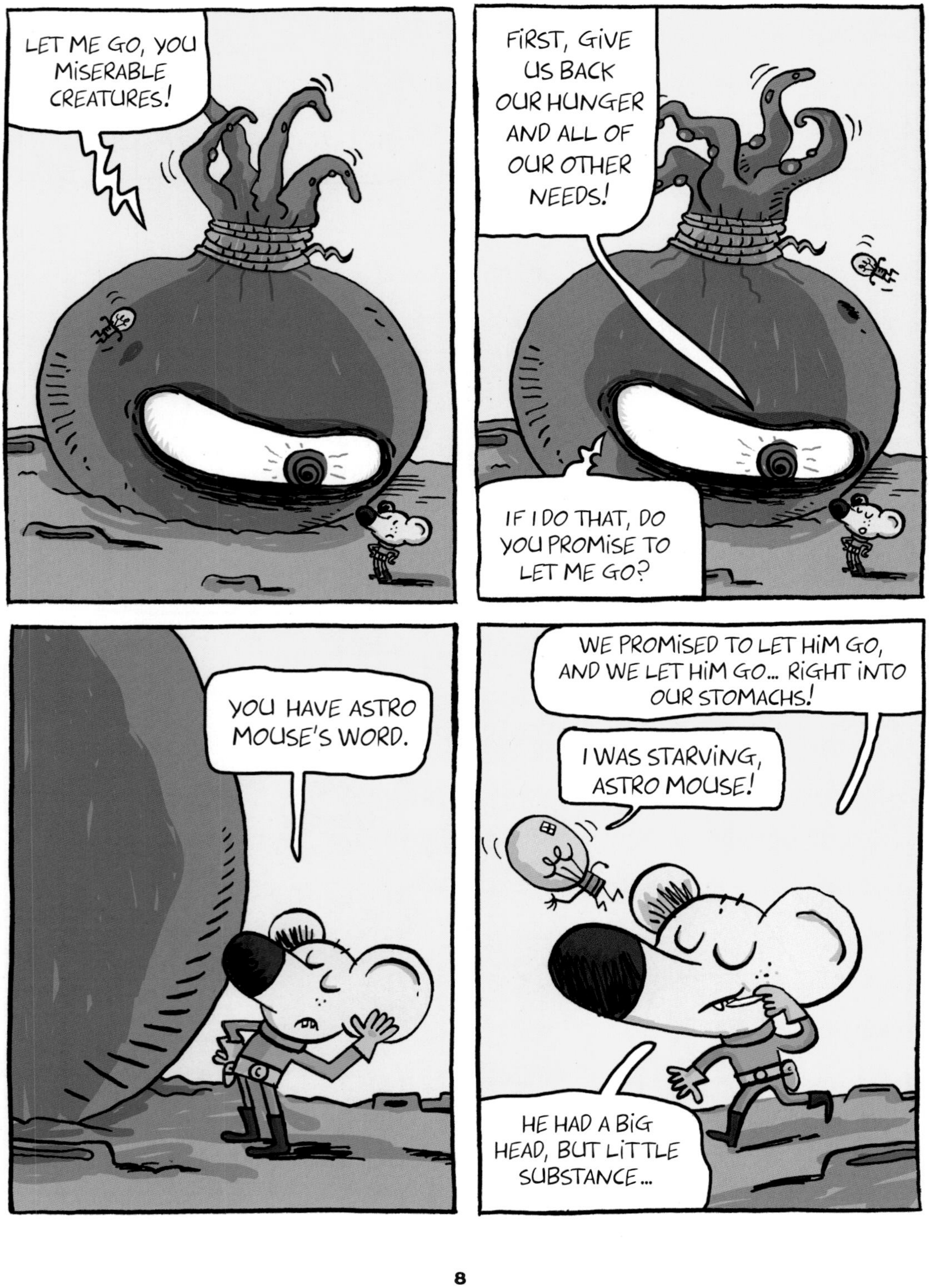
LET ME GO, YOU MISERABLE CREATURES!
FIRST, GIVE US BACK OUR HUNGER AND ALL OF OUR OTHER NEEDS!
IF I DO THAT, DO YOU PROMISE TO LET ME GO?
YOU HAVE ASTRO MOUSE'S WORD.
WE PROMISED TO LET HIM GO, AND WE LET HIM GO... RIGHT INTO OUR STOMACHS!
I WAS STARVING, ASTRO MOUSE!
HE HAD A BIG HEAD, BUT LITTLE SUBSTANCE...

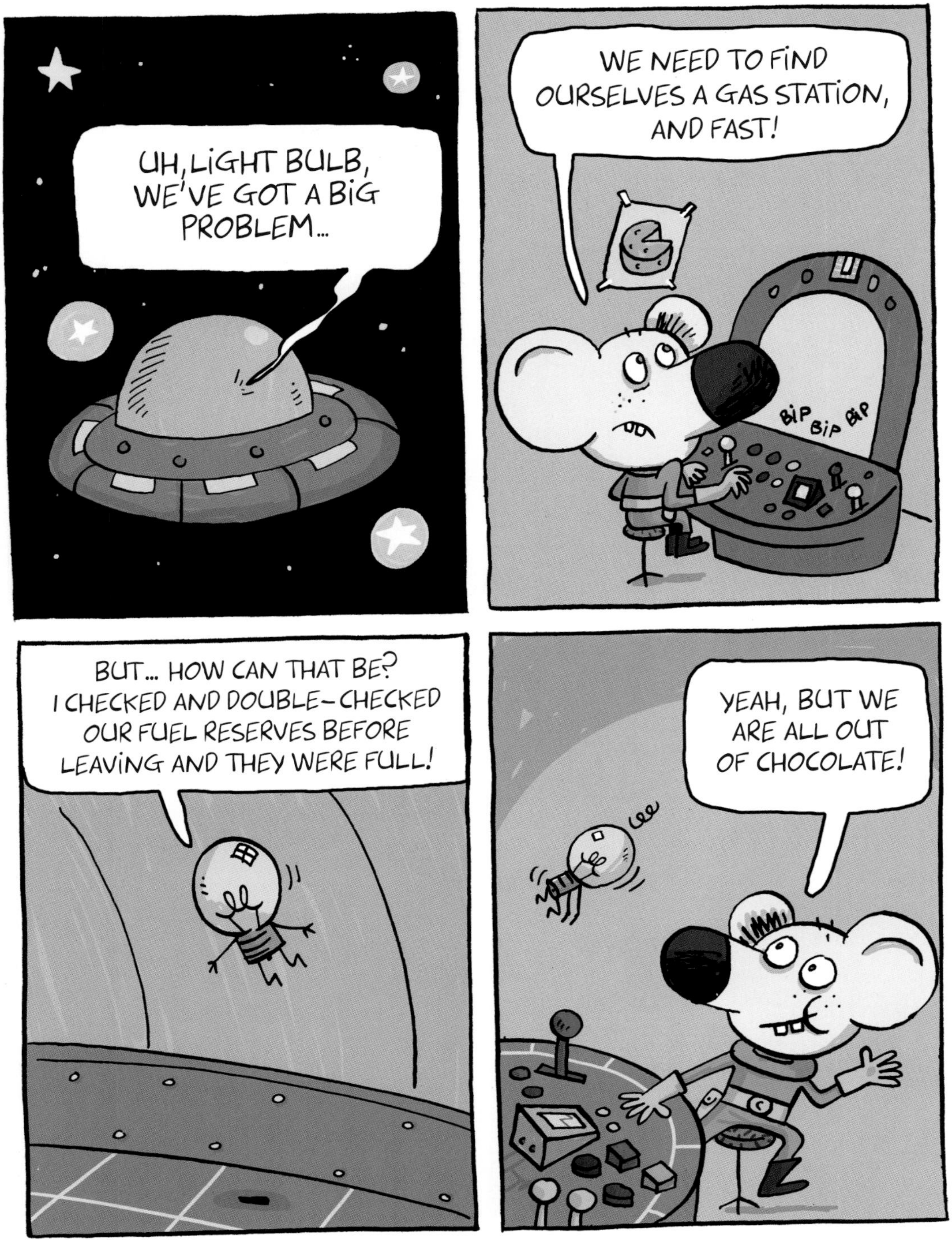
UH, LIGHT BULB, WE'VE GOT A BIG PROBLEM...
WE NEED TO FIND OURSELVES A GAS STATION, AND FAST!
BIP BIP BIP
BUT... HOW CAN THAT BE? I CHECKED AND DOUBLE-CHECKED OUR FUEL RESERVES BEFORE LEAVING AND THEY WERE FULL!
YEAH, BUT WE ARE ALL OUT OF CHOCOLATE!

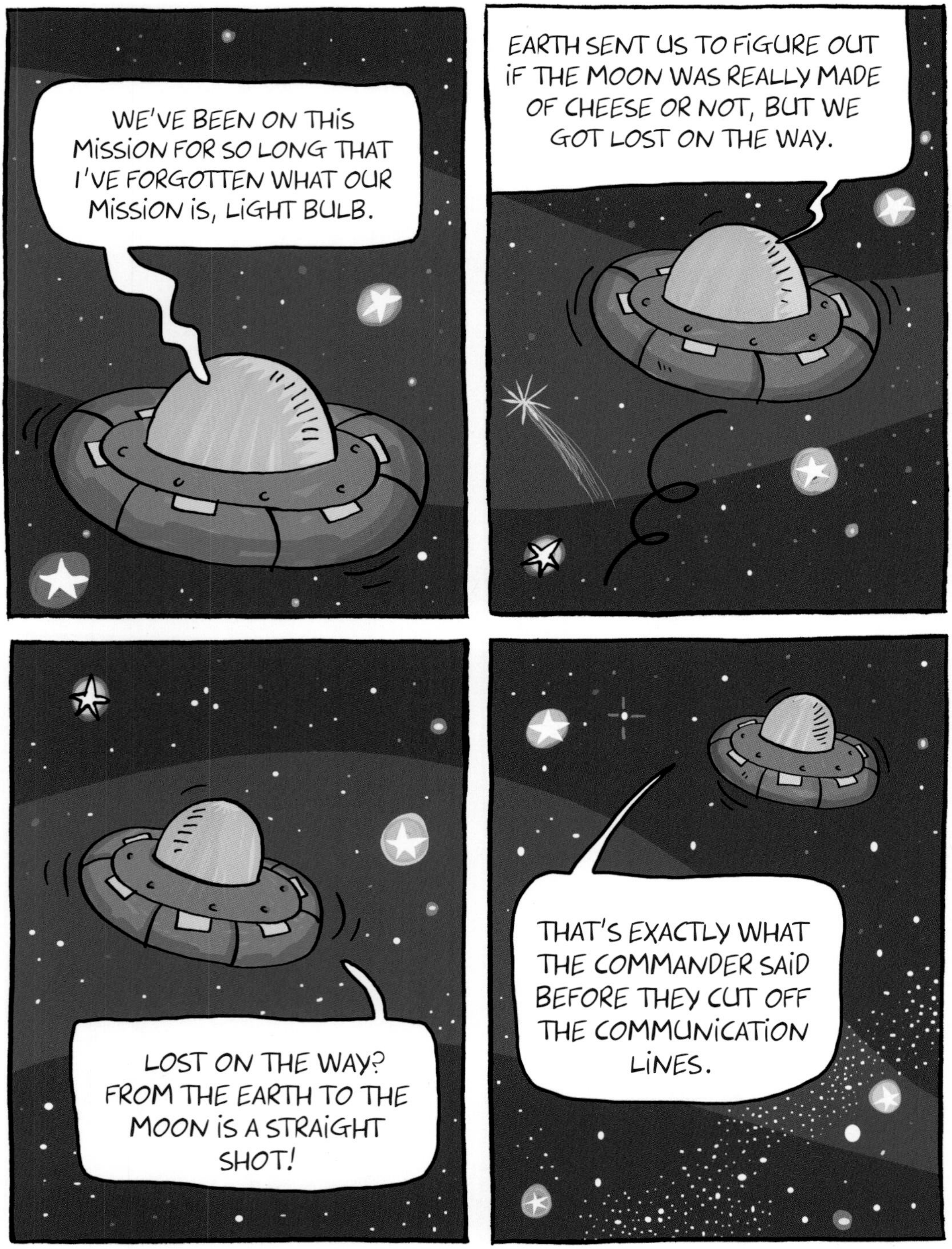
WE'VE BEEN ON THIS MISSION FOR SO LONG THAT I'VE FORGOTTEN WHAT OUR MISSION IS, LIGHT BULB.
EARTH SENT US TO FIGURE OUT IF THE MOON WAS REALLY MADE OF CHEESE OR NOT, BUT WE GOT LOST ON THE WAY.
LOST ON THE WAY? FROM THE EARTH TO THE MOON IS A STRAIGHT SHOT!
THAT'S EXACTLY WHAT THE COMMANDER SAID BEFORE THEY CUT OFF THE COMMUNICATION LINES.

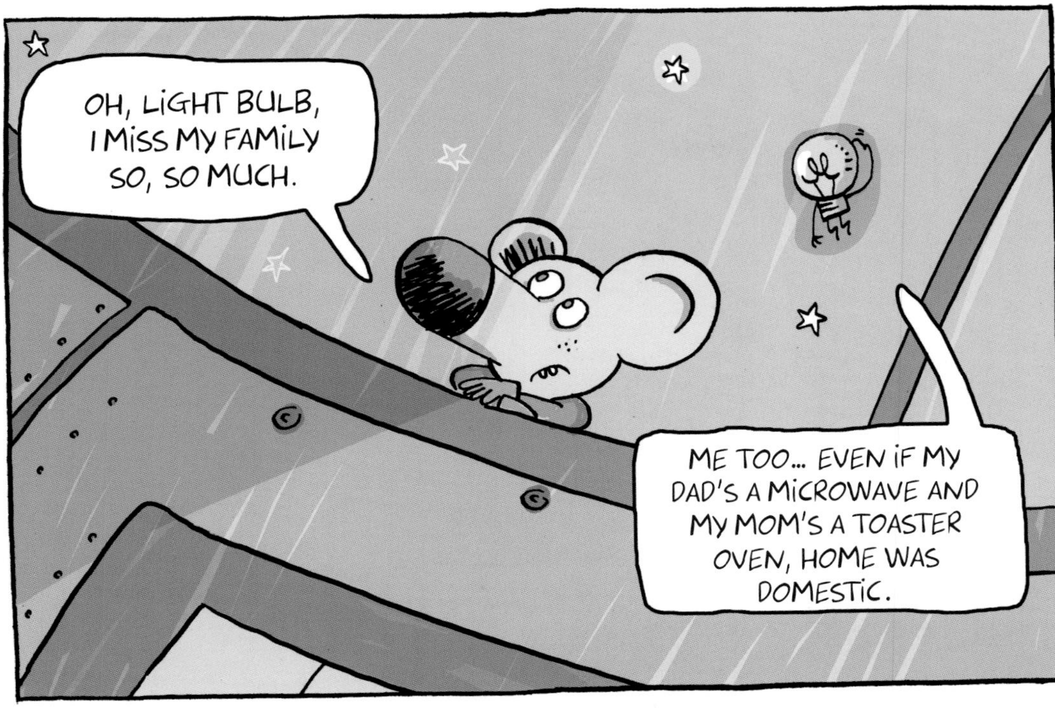
OH, LIGHT BULB, I MISS MY FAMILY SO, SO MUCH.
ME TOO... EVEN IF MY DAD'S A MICROWAVE AND MY MOM'S A TOASTER OVEN, HOME WAS DOMESTIC.

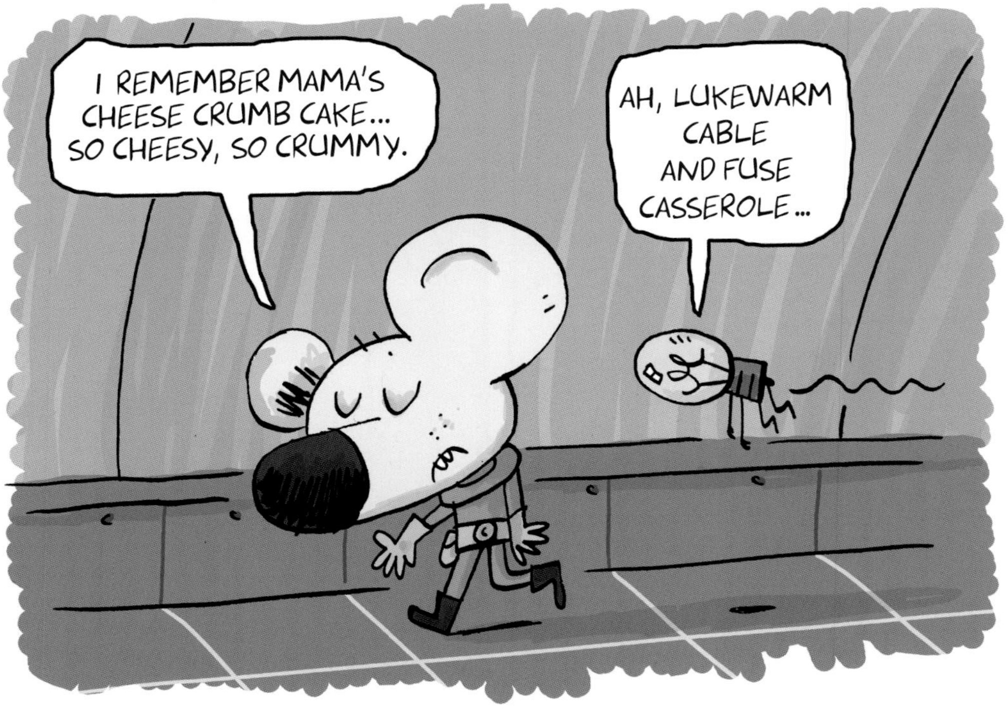
I REMEMBER MAMA'S CHEESE CRUMB CAKE... SO CHEESY, SO CRUMMY.
AH, LUKEWARM CABLE AND FUSE CASSEROLE...

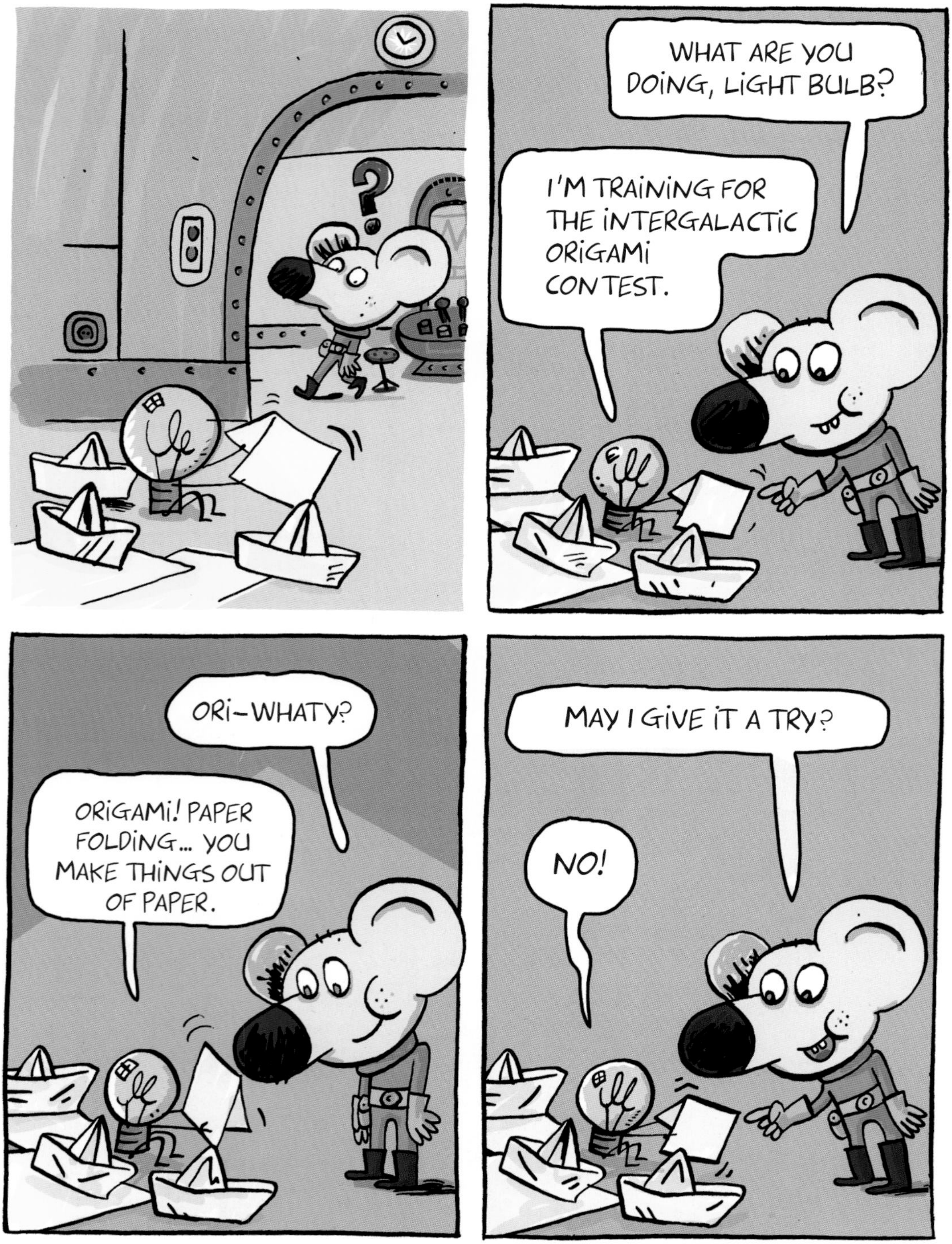
WHAT ARE YOU DOING, LIGHT BULB?
I'M TRAINING FOR THE INTERGALACTIC ORIGAMI CONTEST.
ORI-WHATY?
ORIGAMI! PAPER FOLDING... YOU MAKE THINGS OUT OF PAPER.
MAY I GIVE IT A TRY?
NO!

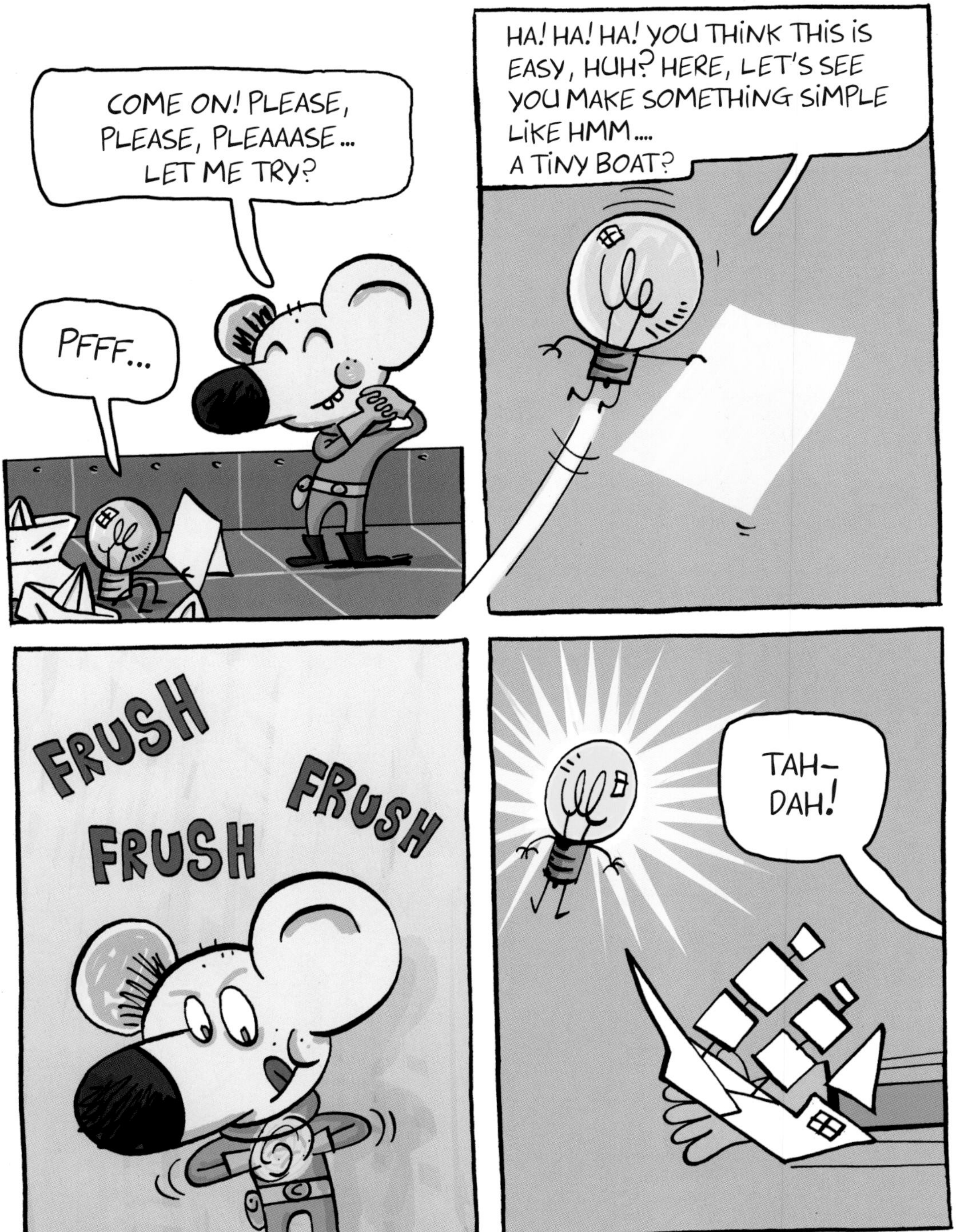
COME ON! PLEASE, PLEASE, PLEAAASE... LET ME TRY?
PFFF...
HA! HA! HA! YOU THINK THIS IS EASY, HUH? HERE, LET'S SEE YOU MAKE SOMETHING SIMPLE LIKE HMM.... A TINY BOAT?
FRUSH
FRUSH
FRUSH
TAH-DAH!

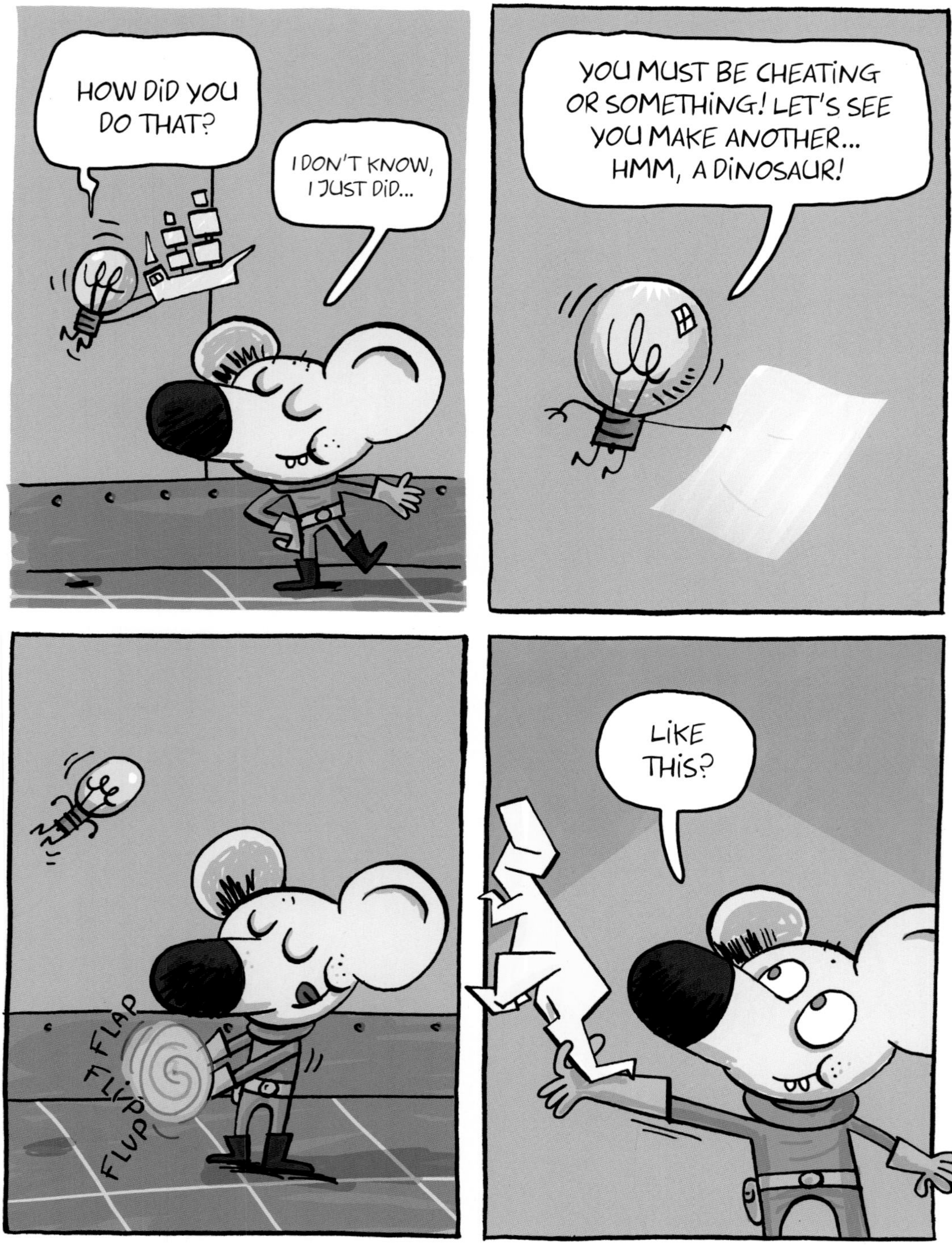
HOW DID YOU DO THAT?
I DON'T KNOW, I JUST DID...
YOU MUST BE CHEATING OR SOMETHING! LET'S SEE YOU MAKE ANOTHER... HMM, A DINOSAUR!
FLAP
FLIP
FLUP
LIKE THIS?

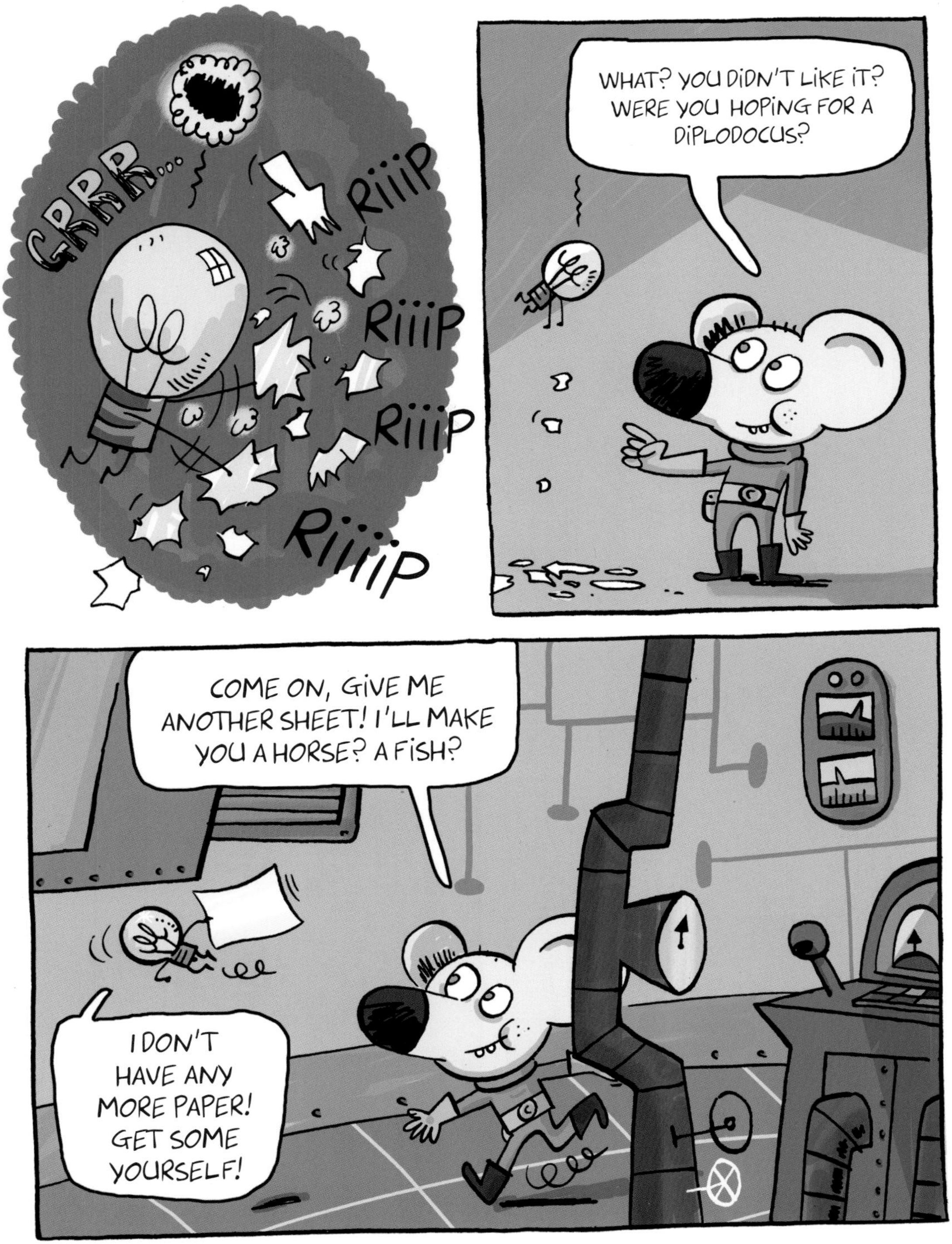
GRRR...
RiiiP
RiiiP
RiiiP
RiiiiP
WHAT? YOU DIDN'T LIKE IT? WERE YOU HOPING FOR A DIPLODOCUS?
COME ON, GIVE ME ANOTHER SHEET! I'LL MAKE YOU A HORSE? A FISH?
I DON'T HAVE ANY MORE PAPER! GET SOME YOURSELF!

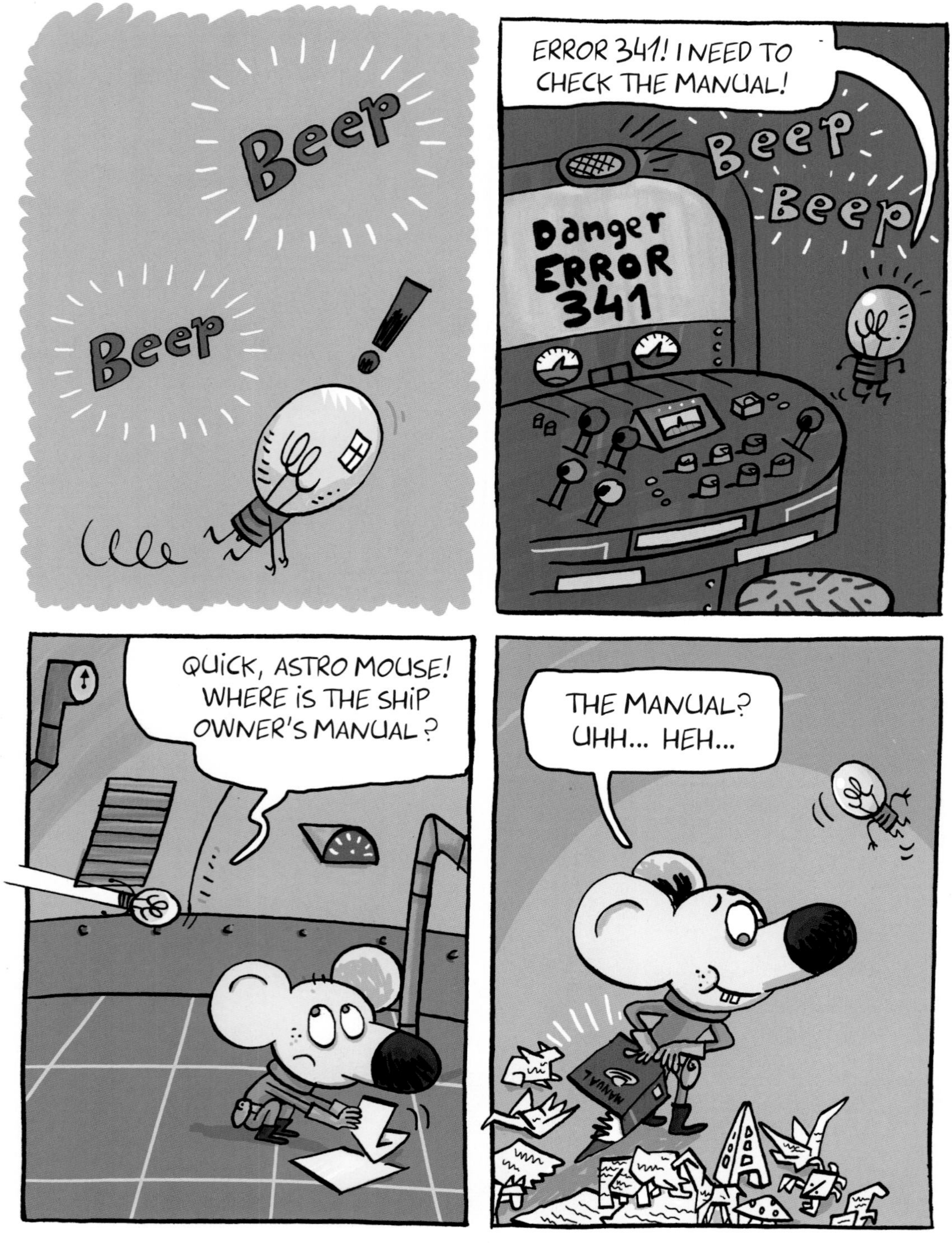
Beep
Beep
ERROR 341! I NEED TO CHECK THE MANUAL!
Beep
Beep
Danger ERROR 341
QUICK, ASTRO MOUSE! WHERE IS THE SHIP OWNER'S MANUAL?
THE MANUAL? UHH... HEH...
MANUAL

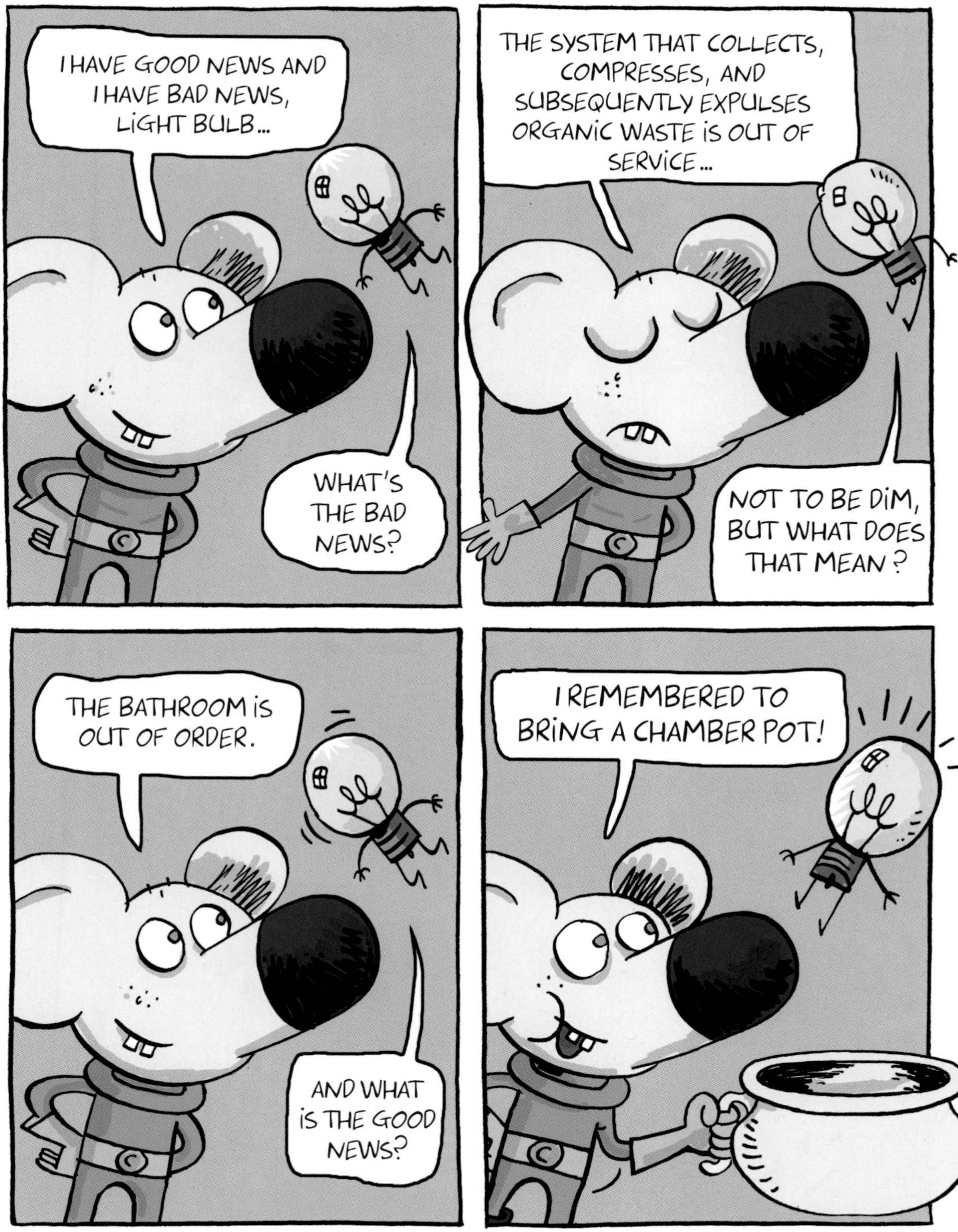
I HAVE GOOD NEWS AND I HAVE BAD NEWS, LIGHT BULB...
WHAT'S THE BAD NEWS?
THE SYSTEM THAT COLLECTS, COMPRESSES, AND SUBSEQUENTLY EXPULSES ORGANIC WASTE IS OUT OF SERVICE...
NOT TO BE DIM, BUT WHAT DOES THAT MEAN ?
THE BATHROOM IS OUT OF ORDER.
AND WHAT IS THE GOOD NEWS?
I REMEMBERED TO BRING A CHAMBER POT!

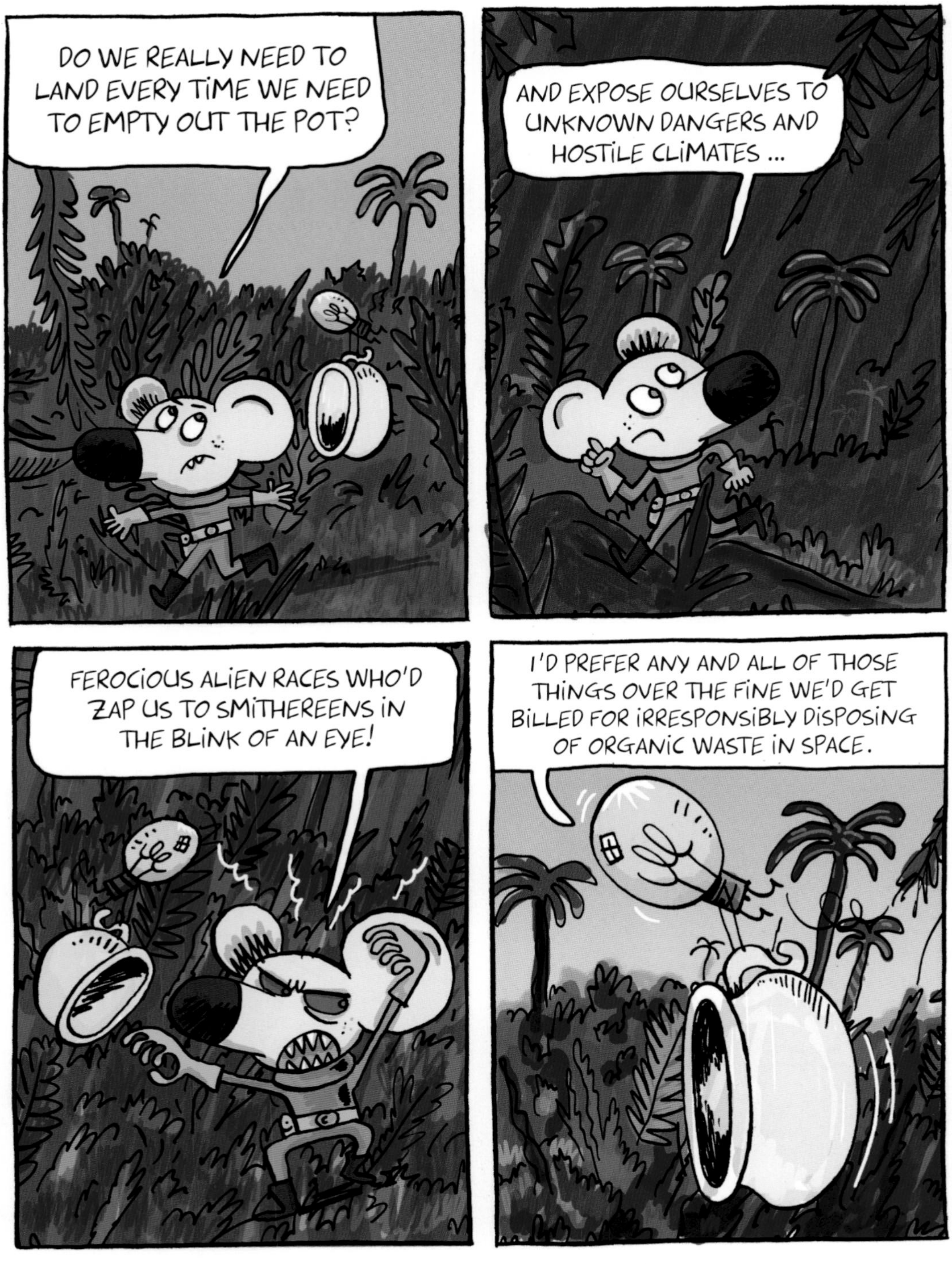
DO WE REALLY NEED TO LAND EVERY TIME WE NEED TO EMPTY OUT THE POT?
AND EXPOSE OURSELVES TO UNKNOWN DANGERS AND HOSTILE CLIMATES ...
FEROCIOUS ALIEN RACES WHO'D ZAP US TO SMITHEREENS IN THE BLINK OF AN EYE!
I'D PREFER ANY AND ALL OF THOSE THINGS OVER THE FINE WE'D GET BILLED FOR IRRESPONSIBLY DISPOSING OF ORGANIC WASTE IN SPACE.

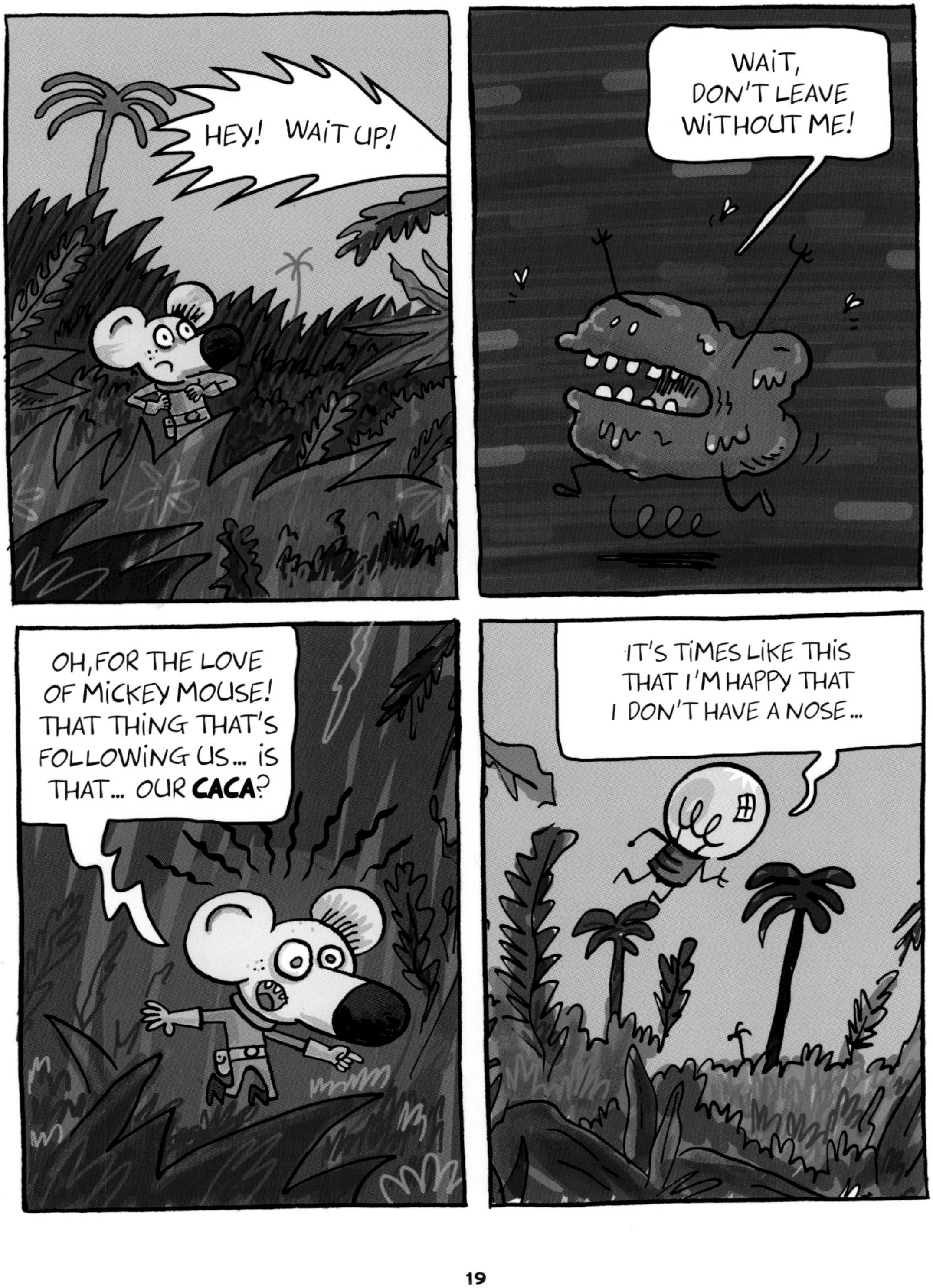
HEY! WAIT UP!
WAIT, DON'T LEAVE WITHOUT ME!
OH, FOR THE LOVE OF MICKEY MOUSE! THAT THING THAT'S FOLLOWING US... IS THAT... OUR **CACA**?
IT'S TIMES LIKE THIS THAT I'M HAPPY THAT I DON'T HAVE A NOSE...

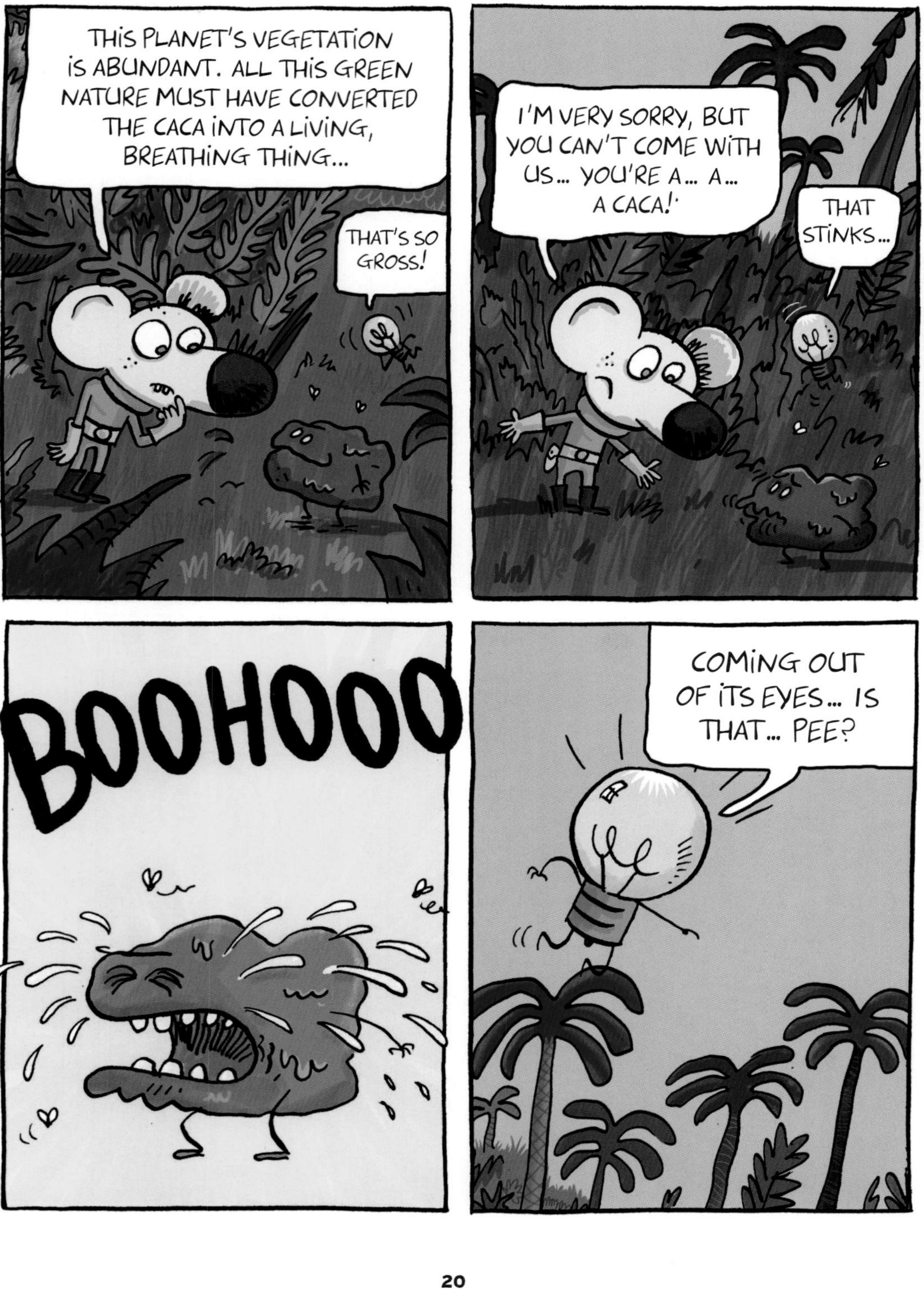
THIS PLANET'S VEGETATION IS ABUNDANT. ALL THIS GREEN NATURE MUST HAVE CONVERTED THE CACA INTO A LIVING, BREATHING THING...
THAT'S SO GROSS!
I'M VERY SORRY, BUT YOU CAN'T COME WITH US... YOU'RE A... A... A CACA!
THAT STINKS...
BOOHOOO
COMING OUT OF ITS EYES... IS THAT... PEE?

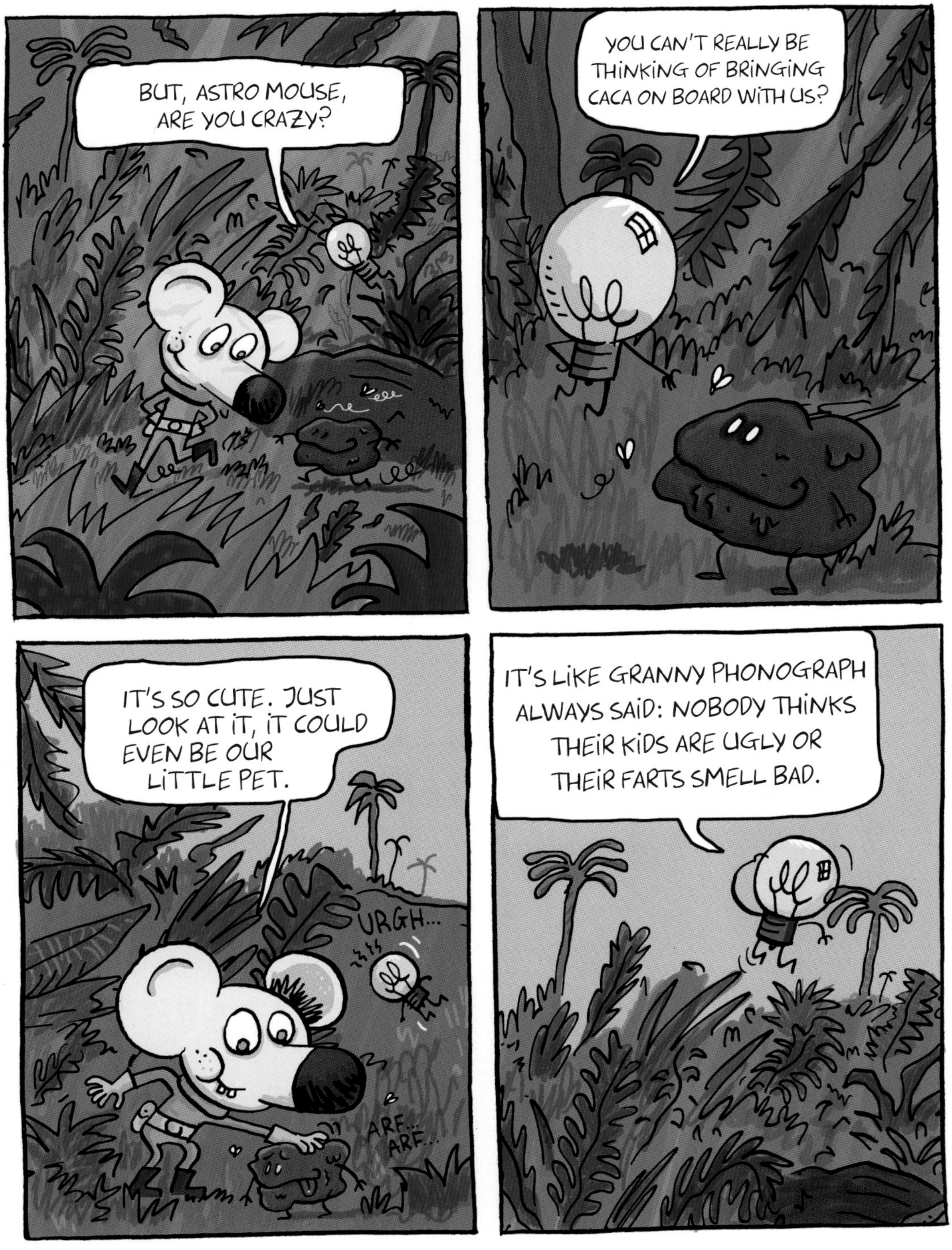
BUT, ASTRO MOUSE, ARE YOU CRAZY?
YOU CAN'T REALLY BE THINKING OF BRINGING CACA ON BOARD WITH US?
IT'S SO CUTE. JUST LOOK AT IT, IT COULD EVEN BE OUR LITTLE PET.
URGH...
ARF... ARF...
IT'S LIKE GRANNY PHONOGRAPH ALWAYS SAID: NOBODY THINKS THEIR KIDS ARE UGLY OR THEIR FARTS SMELL BAD.

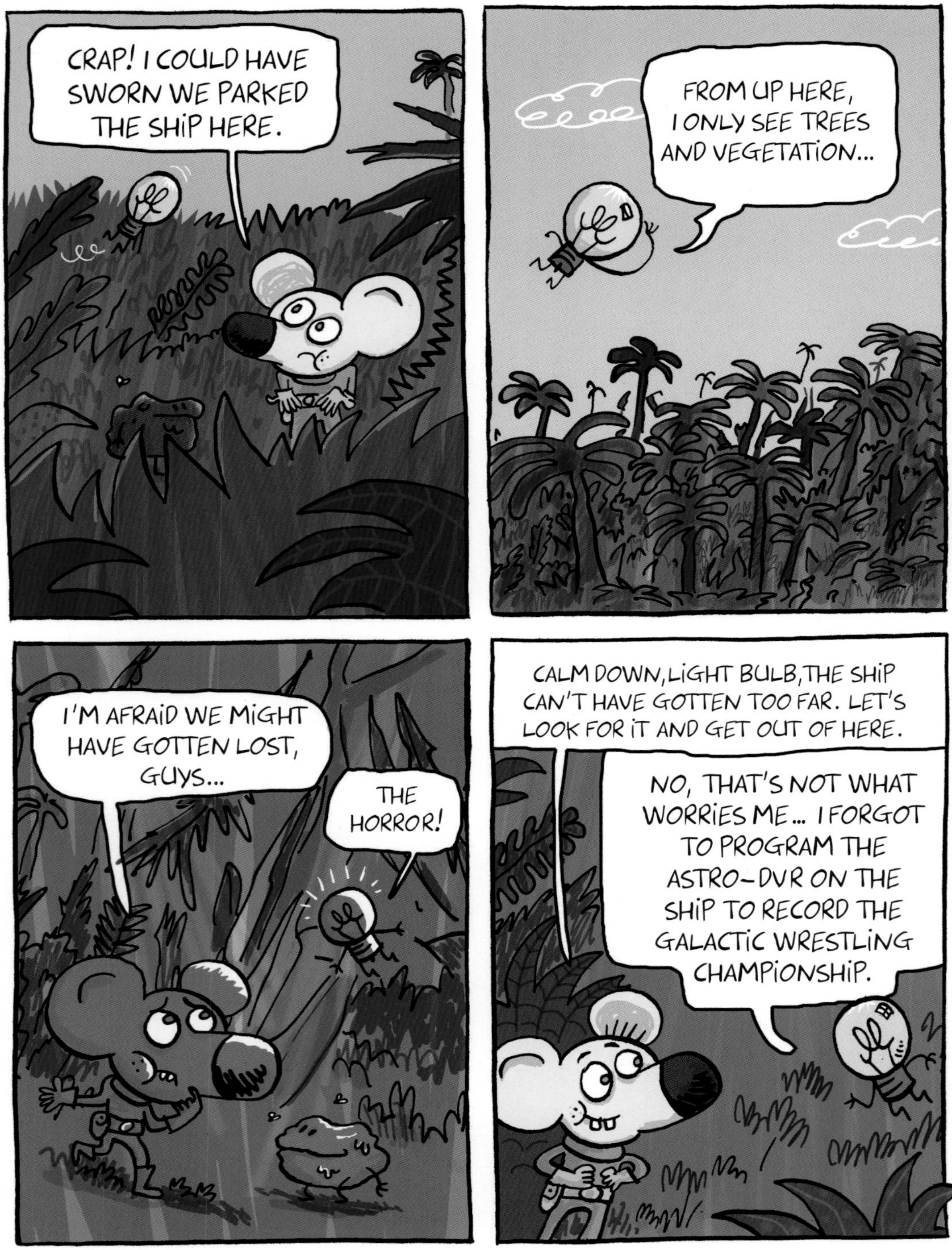
CRAP! I COULD HAVE SWORN WE PARKED THE SHIP HERE.
FROM UP HERE, I ONLY SEE TREES AND VEGETATION...
I'M AFRAID WE MIGHT HAVE GOTTEN LOST, GUYS...
THE HORROR!
CALM DOWN, LIGHT BULB, THE SHIP CAN'T HAVE GOTTEN TOO FAR. LET'S LOOK FOR IT AND GET OUT OF HERE.
NO, THAT'S NOT WHAT WORRIES ME... I FORGOT TO PROGRAM THE ASTRO-DVR ON THE SHIP TO RECORD THE GALACTIC WRESTLING CHAMPIONSHIP.

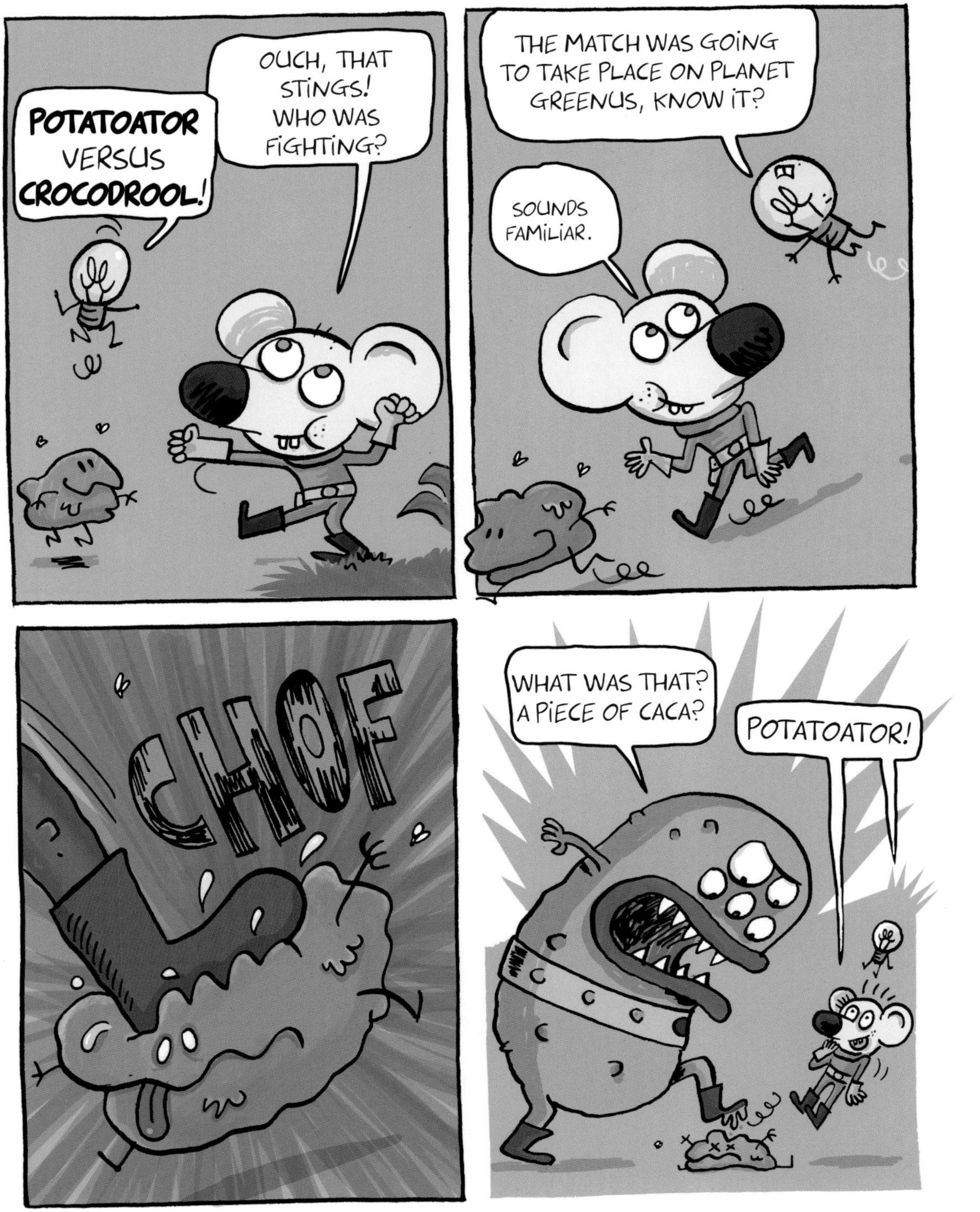
POTATOATOR VERSUS CROCODROOL!
OUCH, THAT STINGS! WHO WAS FIGHTING?
THE MATCH WAS GOING TO TAKE PLACE ON PLANET GREENUS, KNOW IT?
SOUNDS FAMILIAR.
CHOF
WHAT WAS THAT? A PIECE OF CACA?
POTATOATOR!

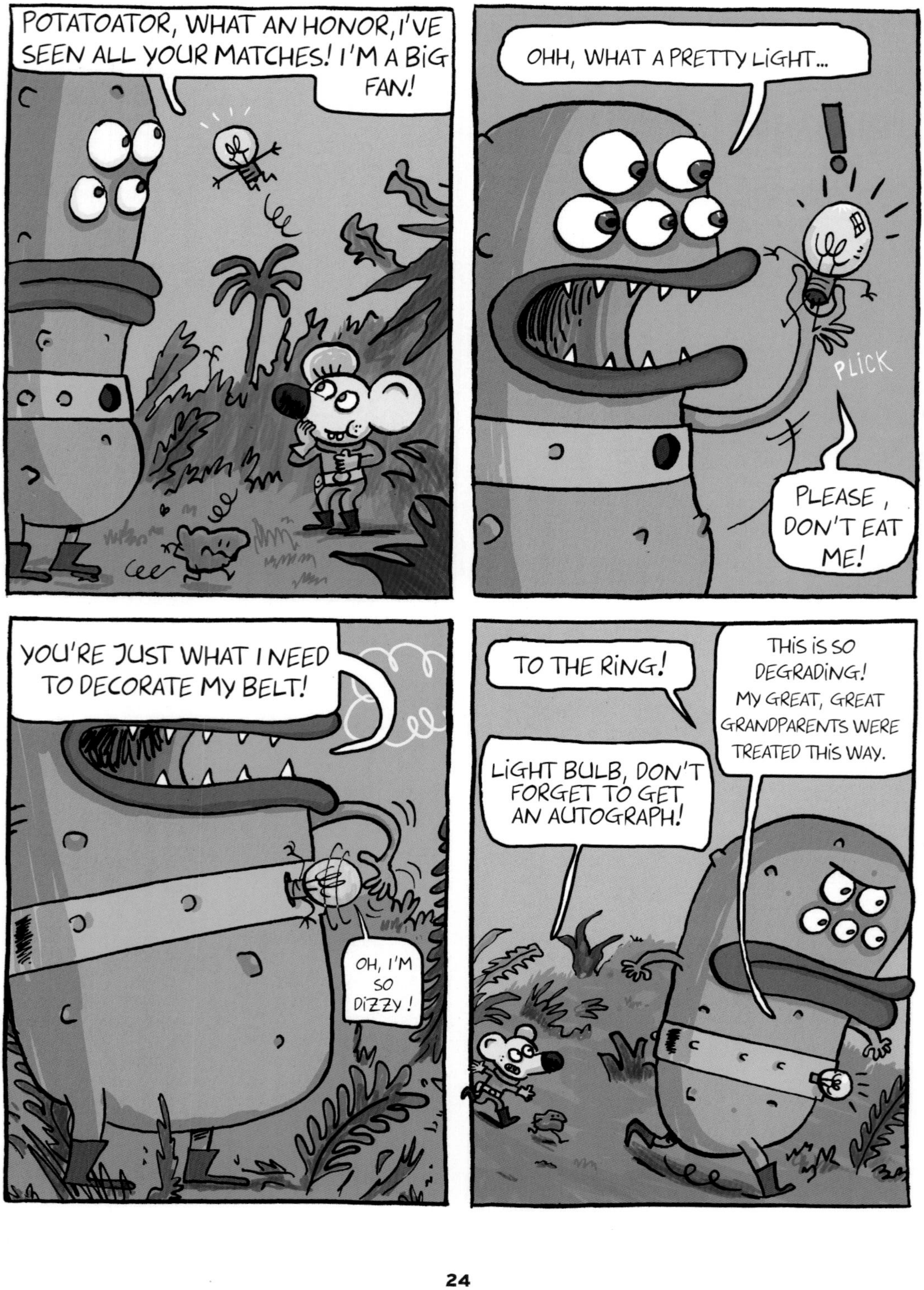
POTATOATOR, WHAT AN HONOR, I'VE SEEN ALL YOUR MATCHES! I'M A BIG FAN!
OHH, WHAT A PRETTY LIGHT...
PLICK
PLEASE, DON'T EAT ME!
YOU'RE JUST WHAT I NEED TO DECORATE MY BELT!
OH, I'M SO DIZZY!
TO THE RING!
THIS IS SO DEGRADING! MY GREAT, GREAT GRANDPARENTS WERE TREATED THIS WAY.
LIGHT BULB, DON'T FORGET TO GET AN AUTOGRAPH!

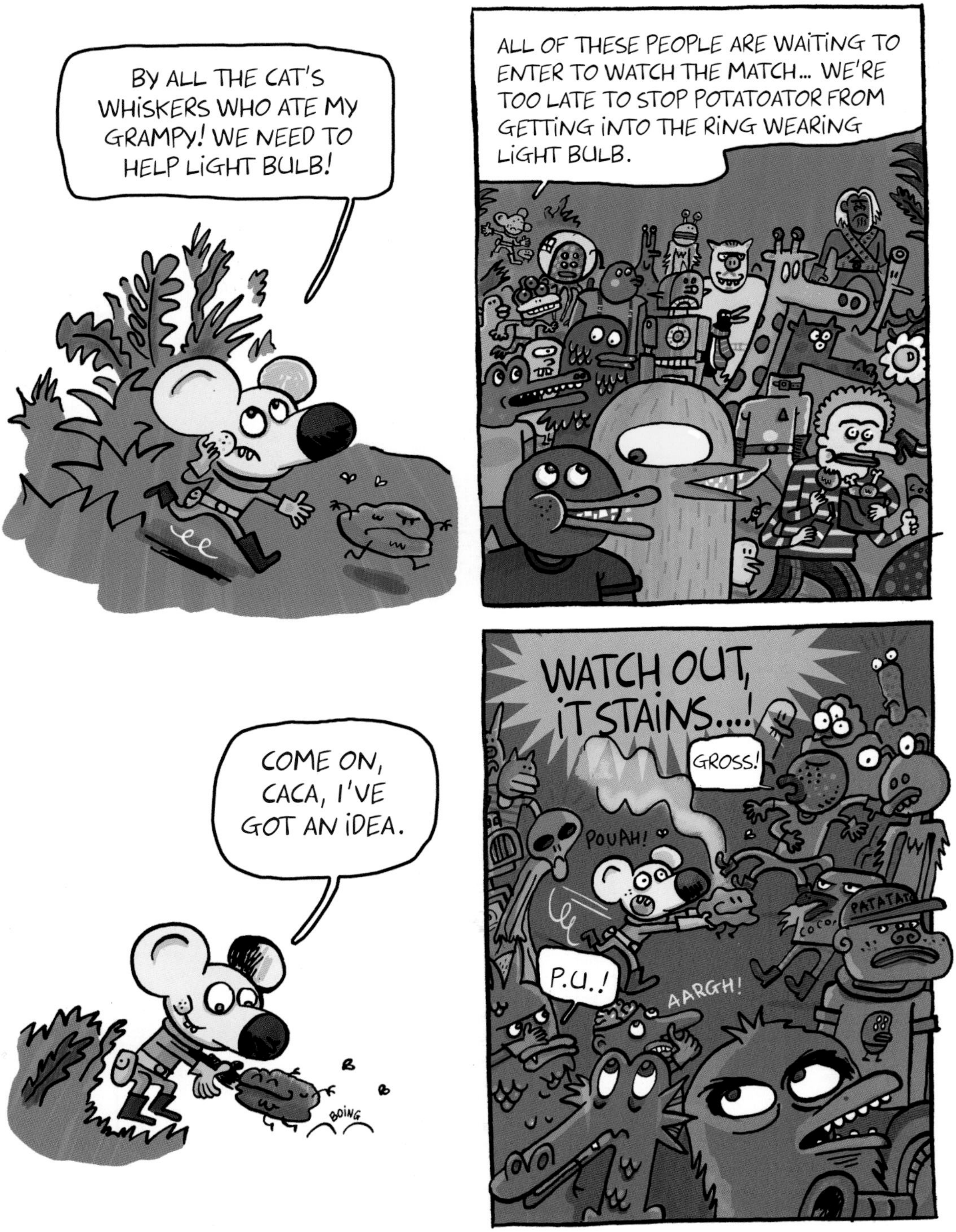
BY ALL THE CAT'S WHISKERS WHO ATE MY GRAMPY! WE NEED TO HELP LIGHT BULB!
ALL OF THESE PEOPLE ARE WAITING TO ENTER TO WATCH THE MATCH... WE'RE TOO LATE TO STOP POTATOATOR FROM GETTING INTO THE RING WEARING LIGHT BULB.
COME ON, CACA, I'VE GOT AN IDEA.
BOING
WATCH OUT, IT STAINS...!
GROSS!
POUAH!
P.U.!
AARGH!

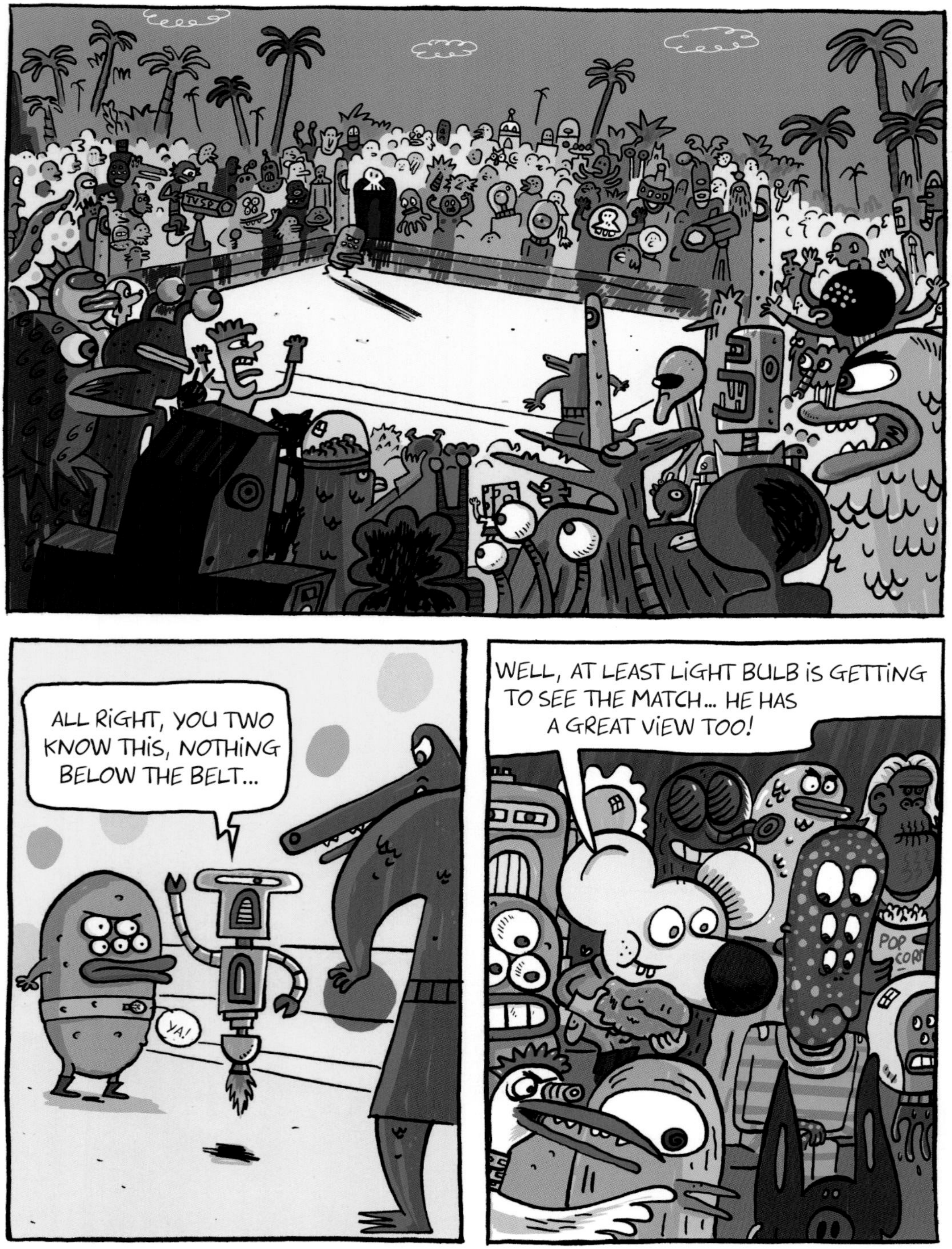
ALL RIGHT, YOU TWO KNOW THIS, NOTHING BELOW THE BELT...
YA!
WELL, AT LEAST LIGHT BULB IS GETTING TO SEE THE MATCH... HE HAS A GREAT VIEW TOO!

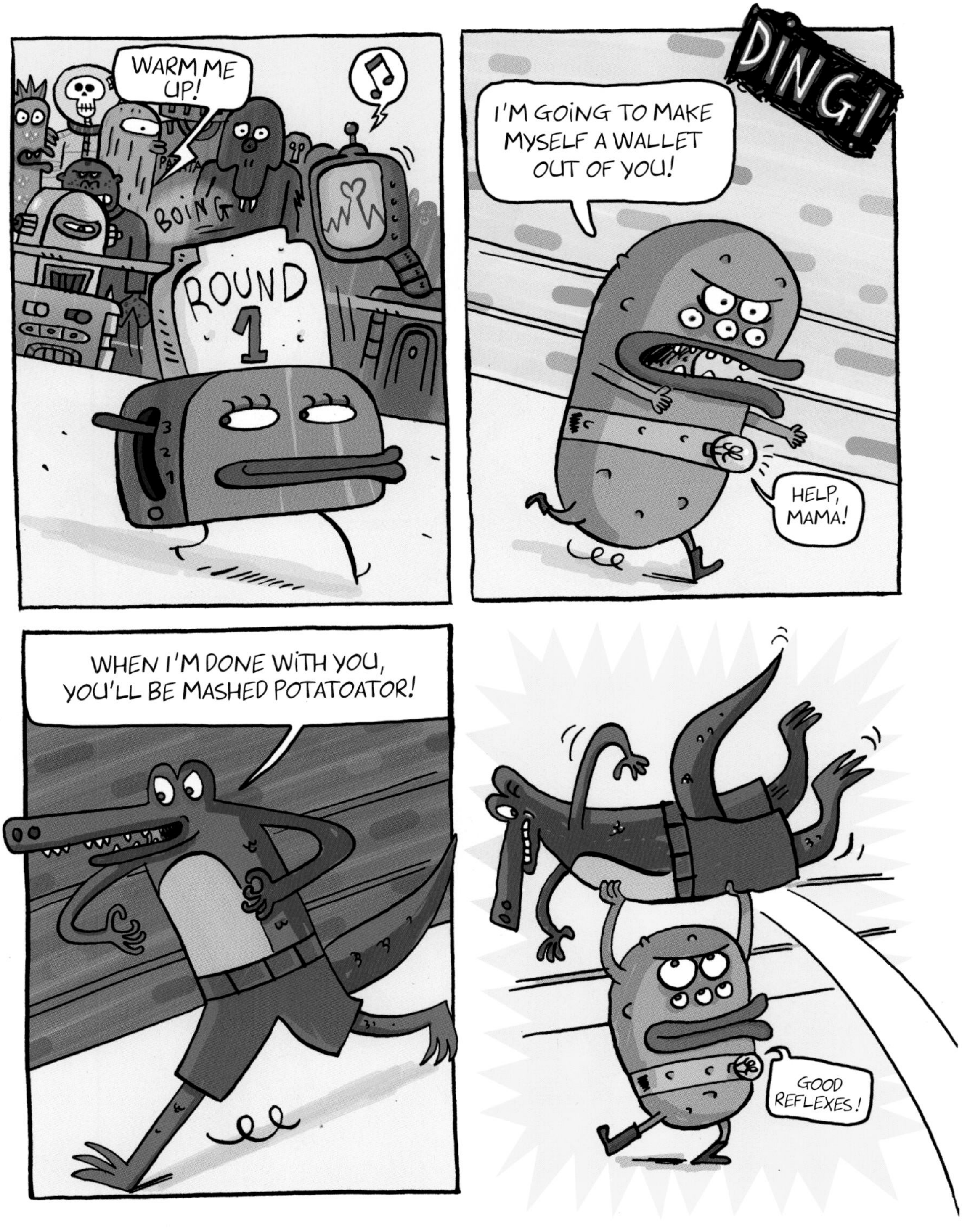
WARM ME UP!
BOING
ROUND 1
DING!
I'M GOING TO MAKE MYSELF A WALLET OUT OF YOU!
HELP, MAMA!
WHEN I'M DONE WITH YOU, YOU'LL BE MASHED POTATOATOR!
GOOD REFLEXES!

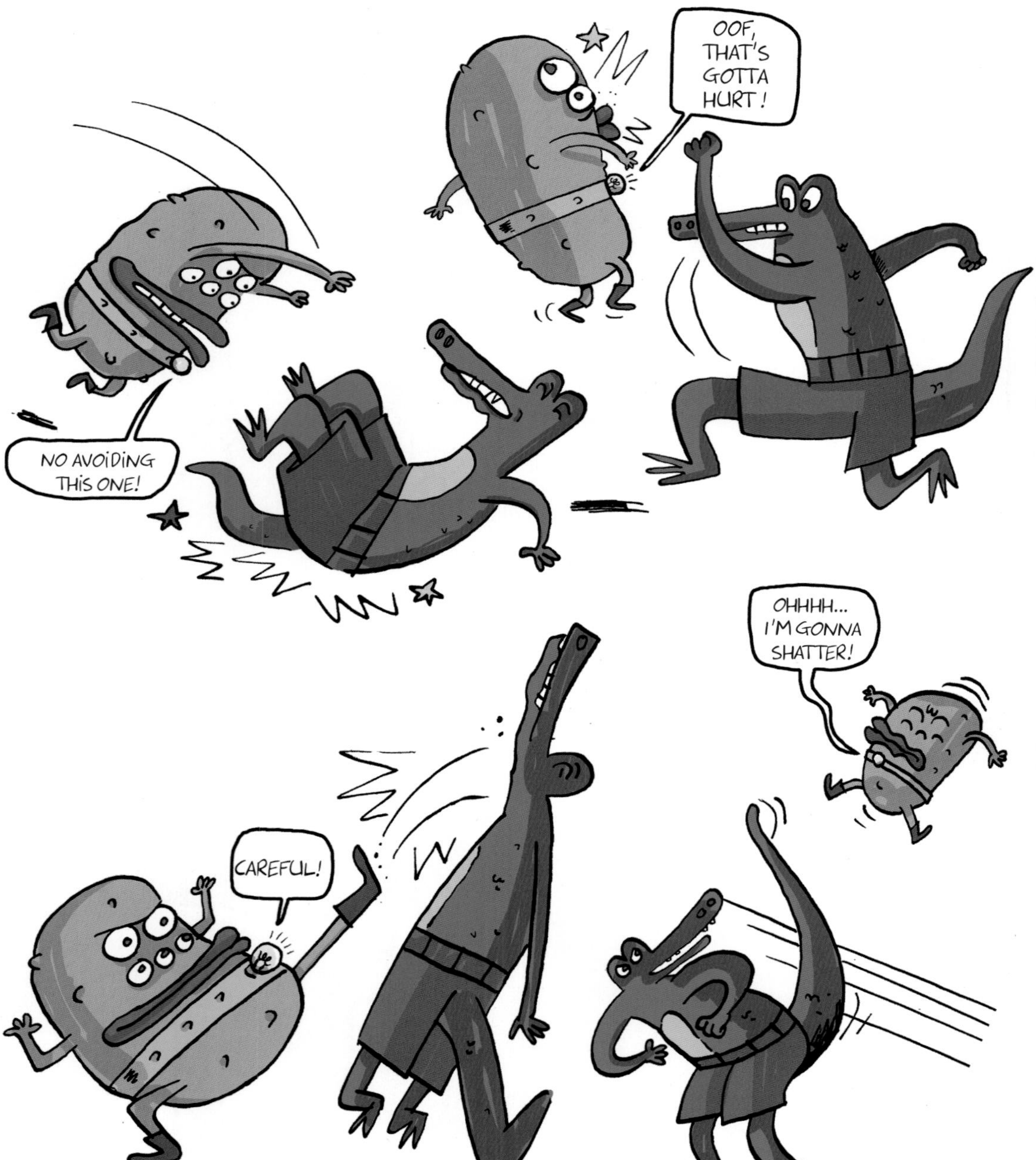
OOF, THAT'S GOTTA HURT!
NO AVOIDING THIS ONE!
OHHHH... I'M GONNA SHATTER!
CAREFUL!

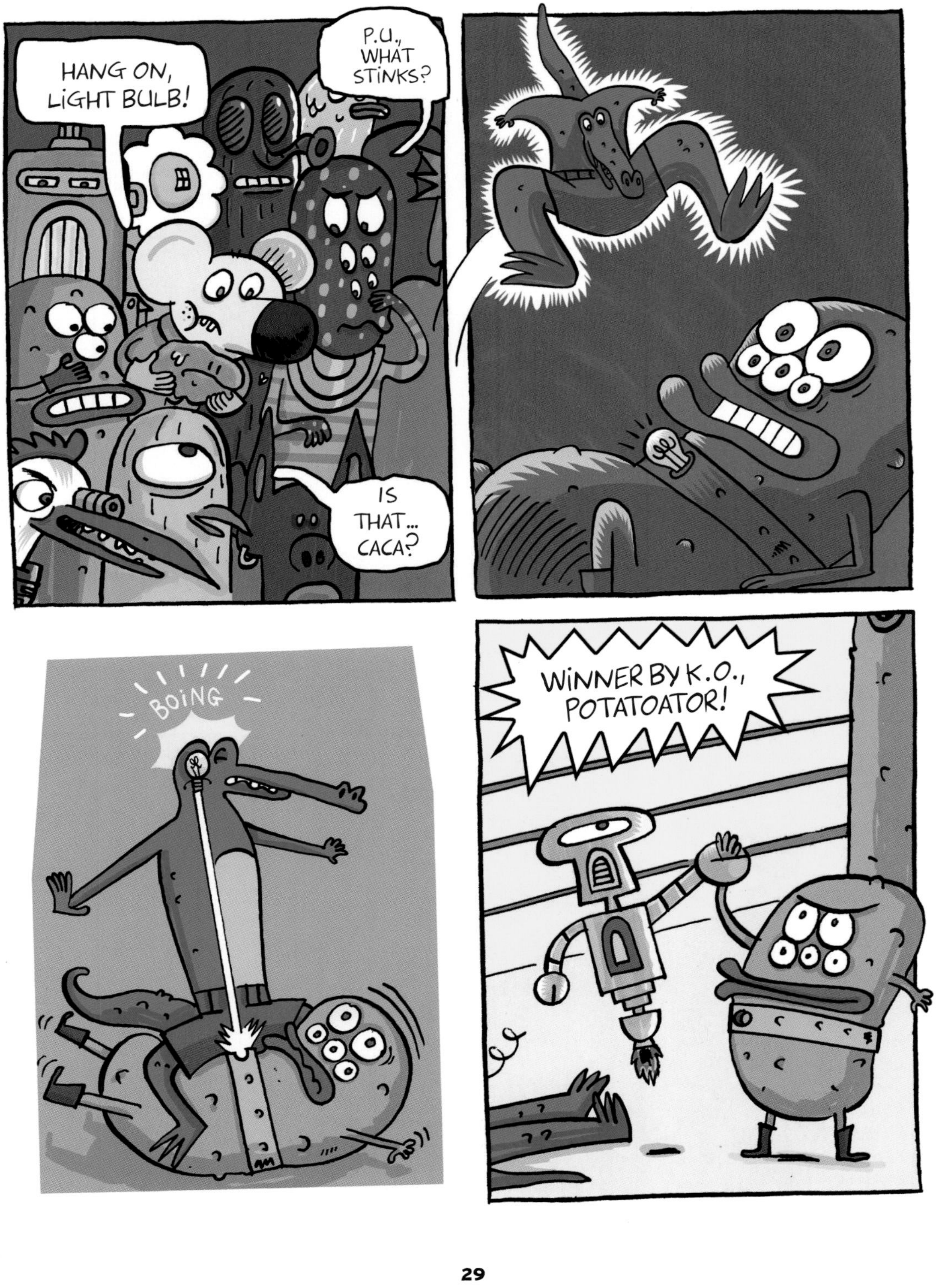

HANG ON, LIGHT BULB!
P.U., WHAT STINKS?
IS THAT... CACA?
BOING
WINNER BY K.O., POTATOATOR!

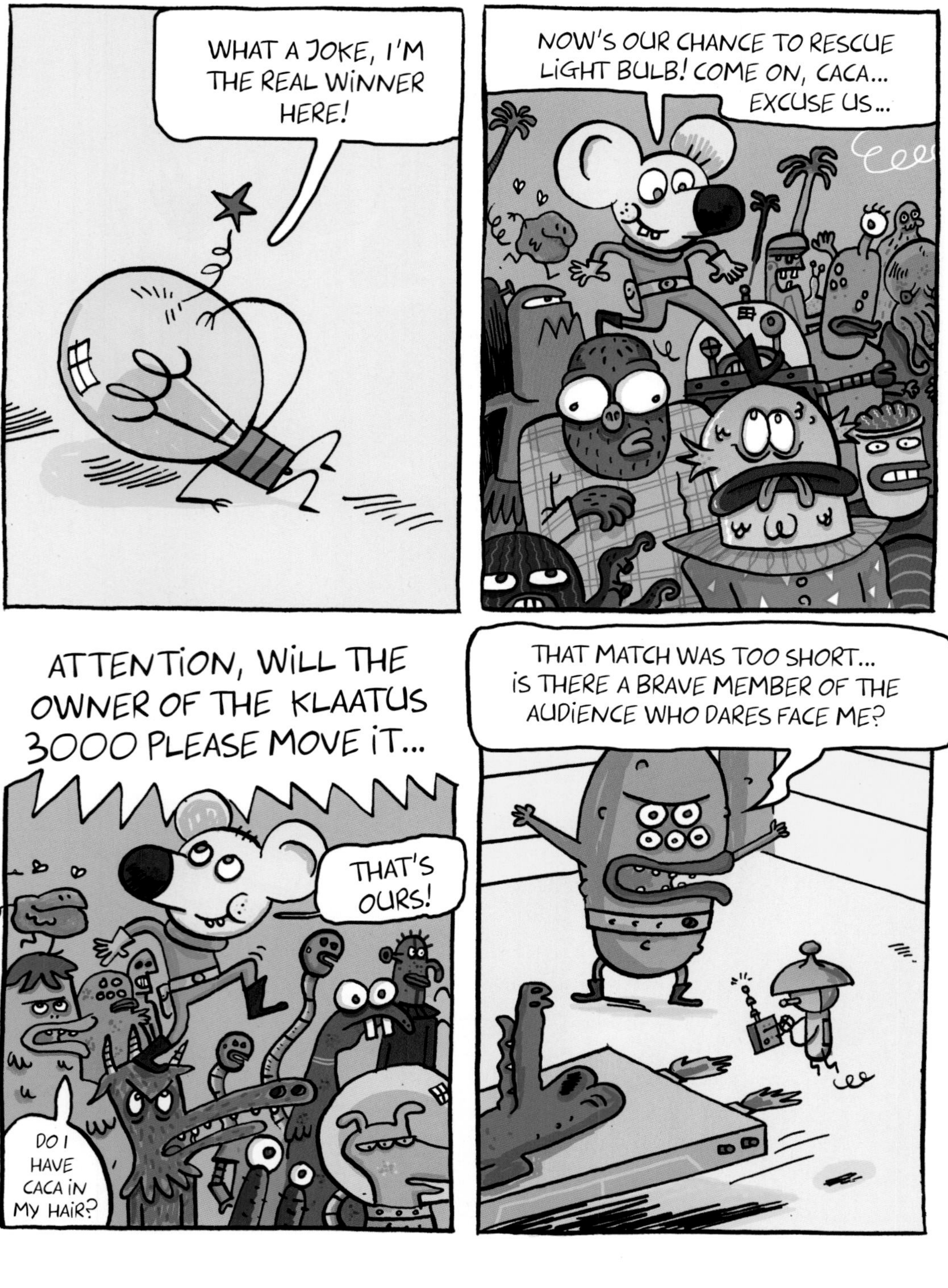
WHAT A JOKE, I'M THE REAL WINNER HERE!
NOW'S OUR CHANCE TO RESCUE LIGHT BULB! COME ON, CACA... EXCUSE US...
ATTENTION, WILL THE OWNER OF THE KLAATUS 3000 PLEASE MOVE IT...
THAT'S OURS!
DO I HAVE CACA IN MY HAIR?
THAT MATCH WAS TOO SHORT... IS THERE A BRAVE MEMBER OF THE AUDIENCE WHO DARES FACE ME?

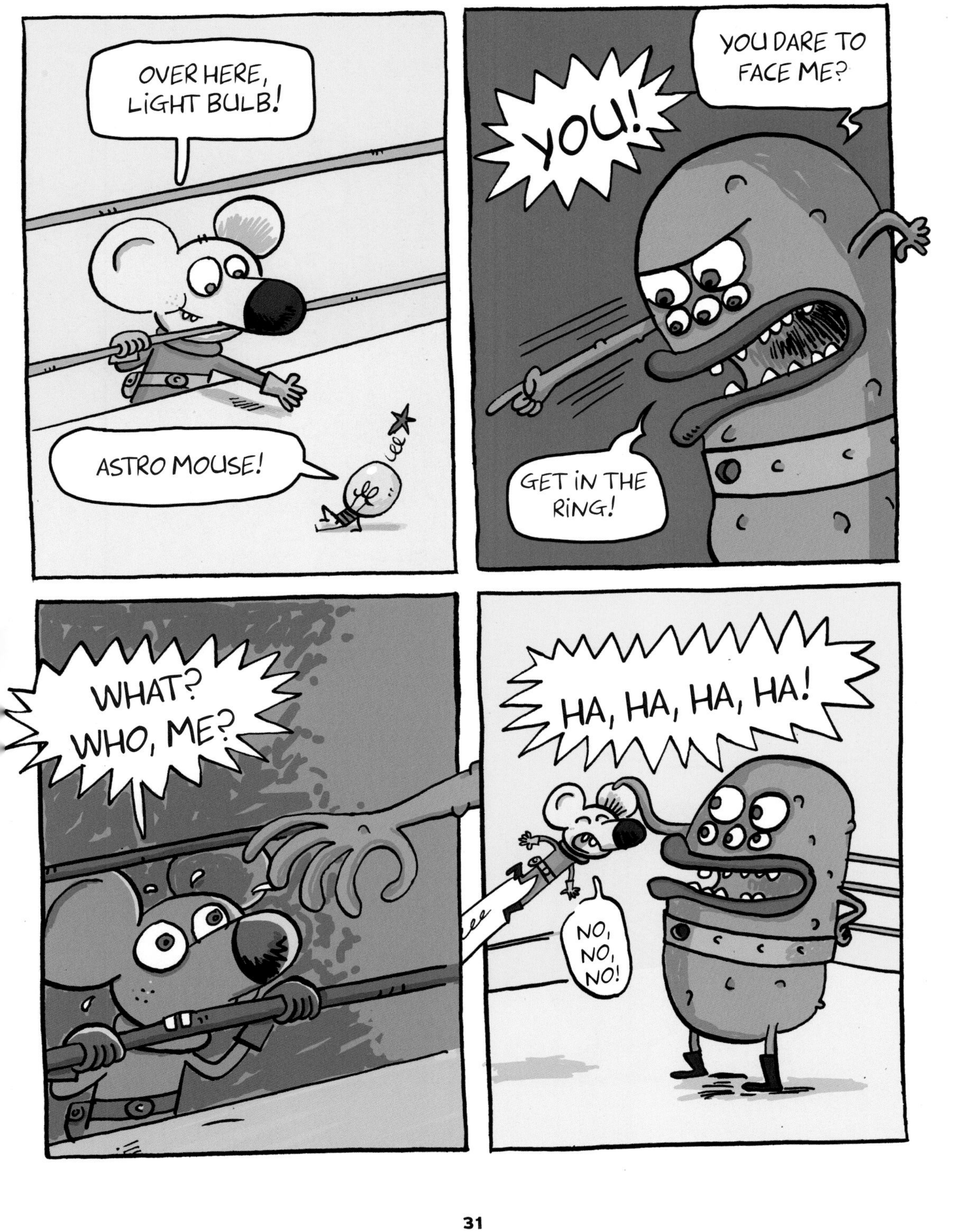
OVER HERE, LIGHT BULB!
ASTRO MOUSE!
YOU!
YOU DARE TO FACE ME?
GET IN THE RING!
WHAT? WHO, ME?
HA, HA, HA, HA!
NO, NO, NO!

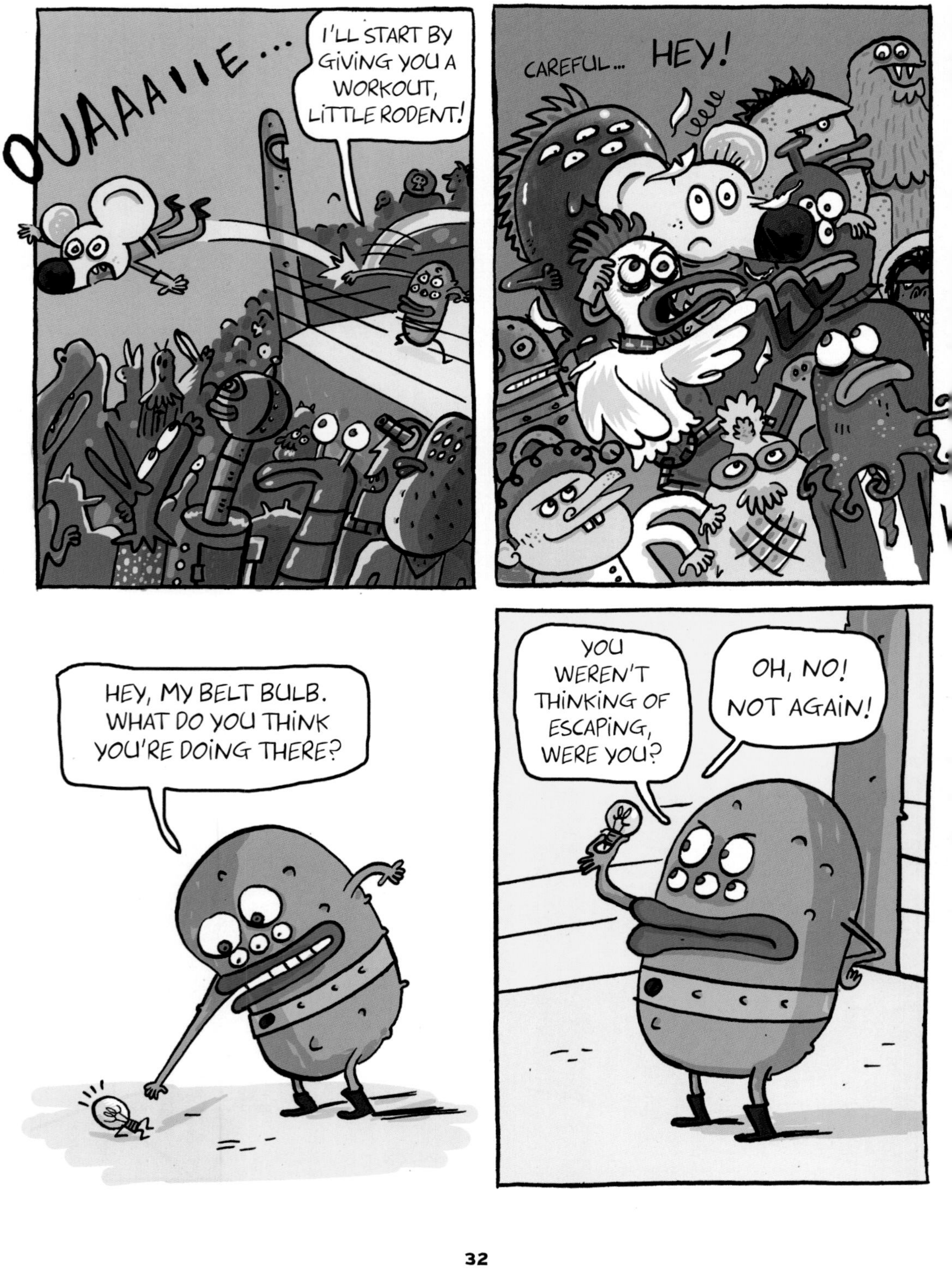
OUAAAIIIE...
I'LL START BY GIVING YOU A WORKOUT, LITTLE RODENT!
CAREFUL...
HEY!
HEY, MY BELT BULB. WHAT DO YOU THINK YOU'RE DOING THERE?
YOU WEREN'T THINKING OF ESCAPING, WERE YOU?
OH, NO! NOT AGAIN!

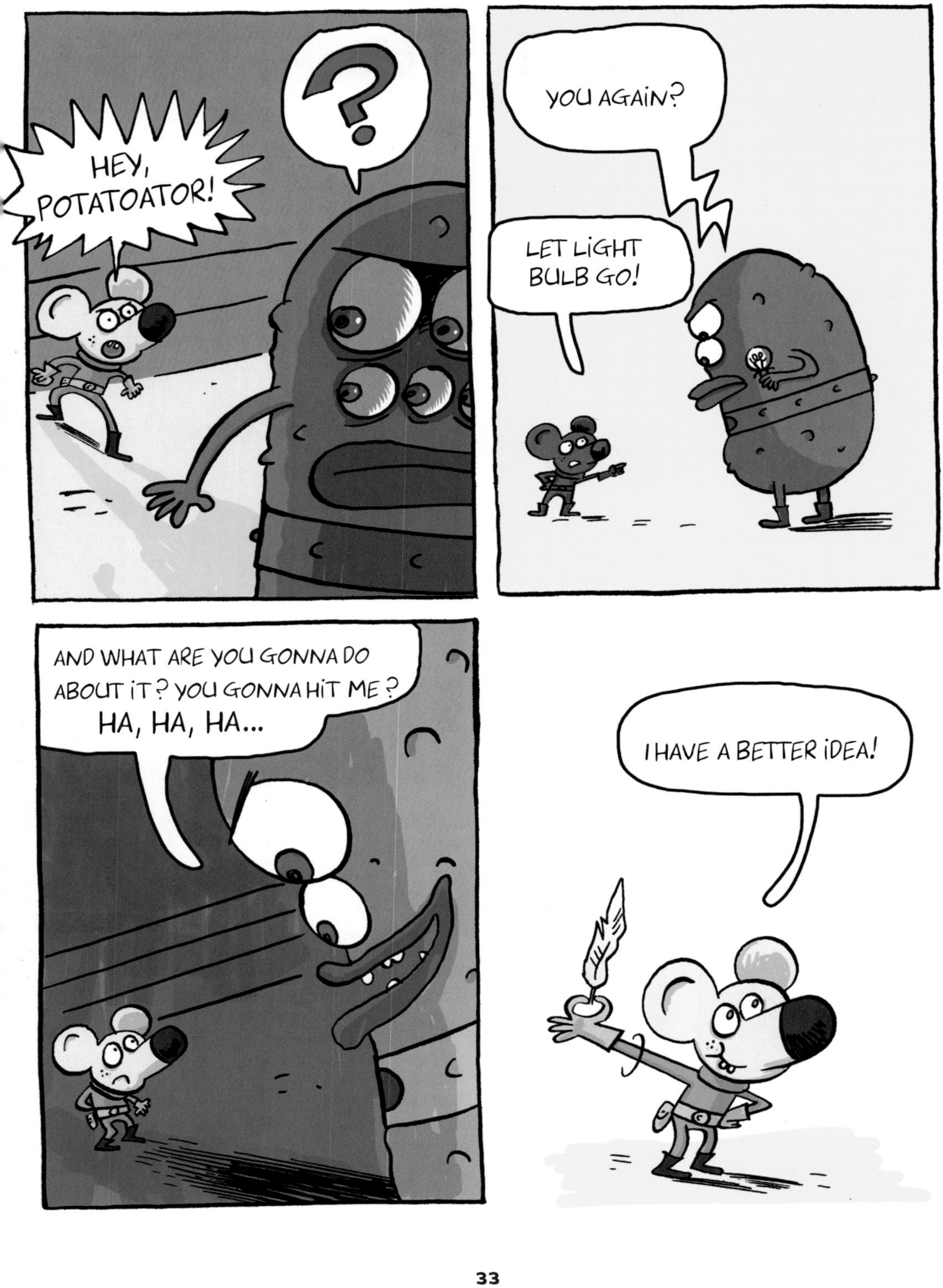
HEY, POTATOATOR!
?
YOU AGAIN?
LET LIGHT BULB GO!
AND WHAT ARE YOU GONNA DO ABOUT IT? YOU GONNA HIT ME? HA, HA, HA...
I HAVE A BETTER IDEA!

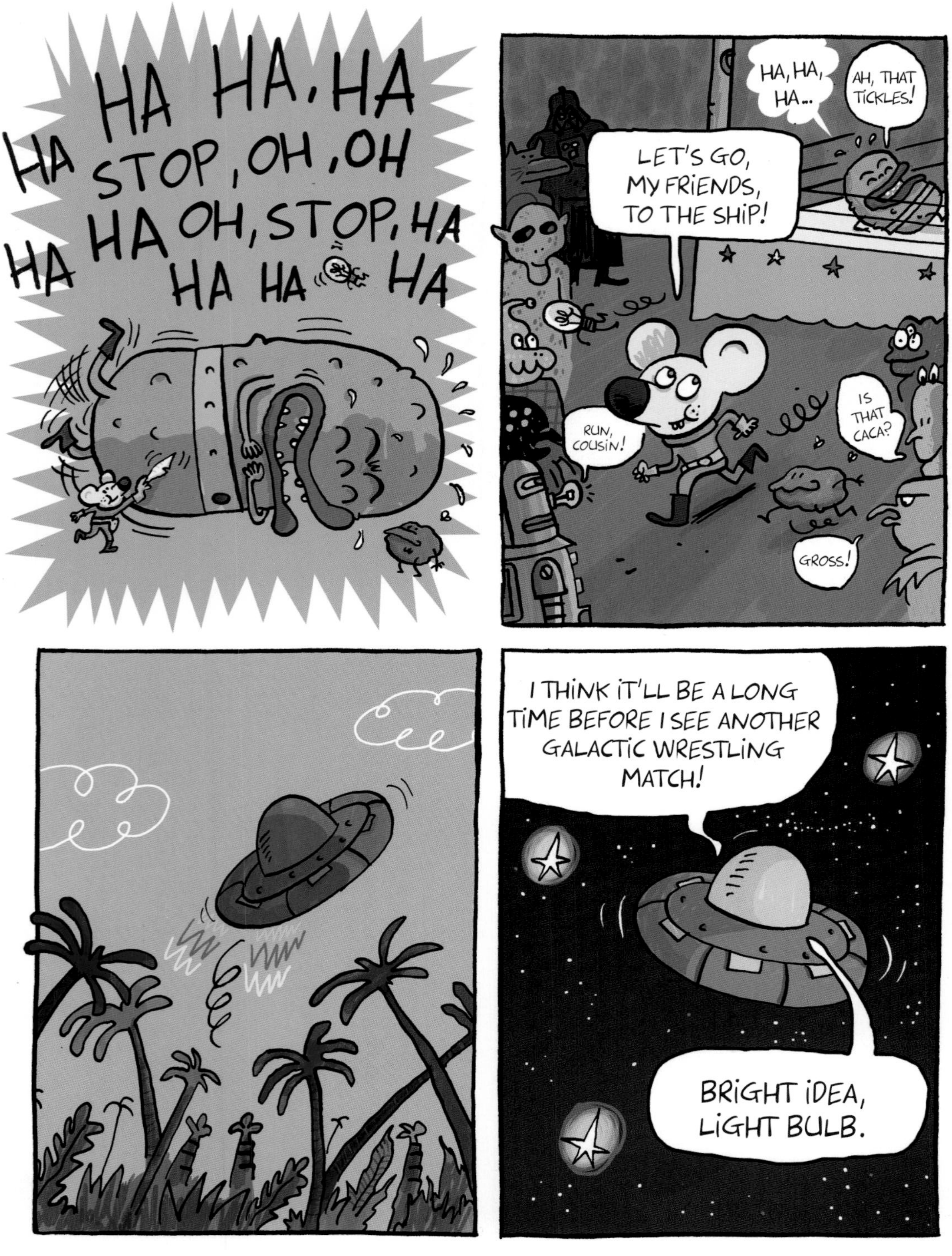
HA HA HA, HA
STOP, OH, OH
HA HA OH, STOP, HA
HA HA HA
HA, HA, HA...
AH, THAT TICKLES!
LET'S GO, MY FRIENDS, TO THE SHIP!
RUN, COUSIN!
IS THAT CACA?
GROSS!
I THINK IT'LL BE A LONG TIME BEFORE I SEE ANOTHER GALACTIC WRESTLING MATCH!
BRIGHT IDEA, LIGHT BULB.

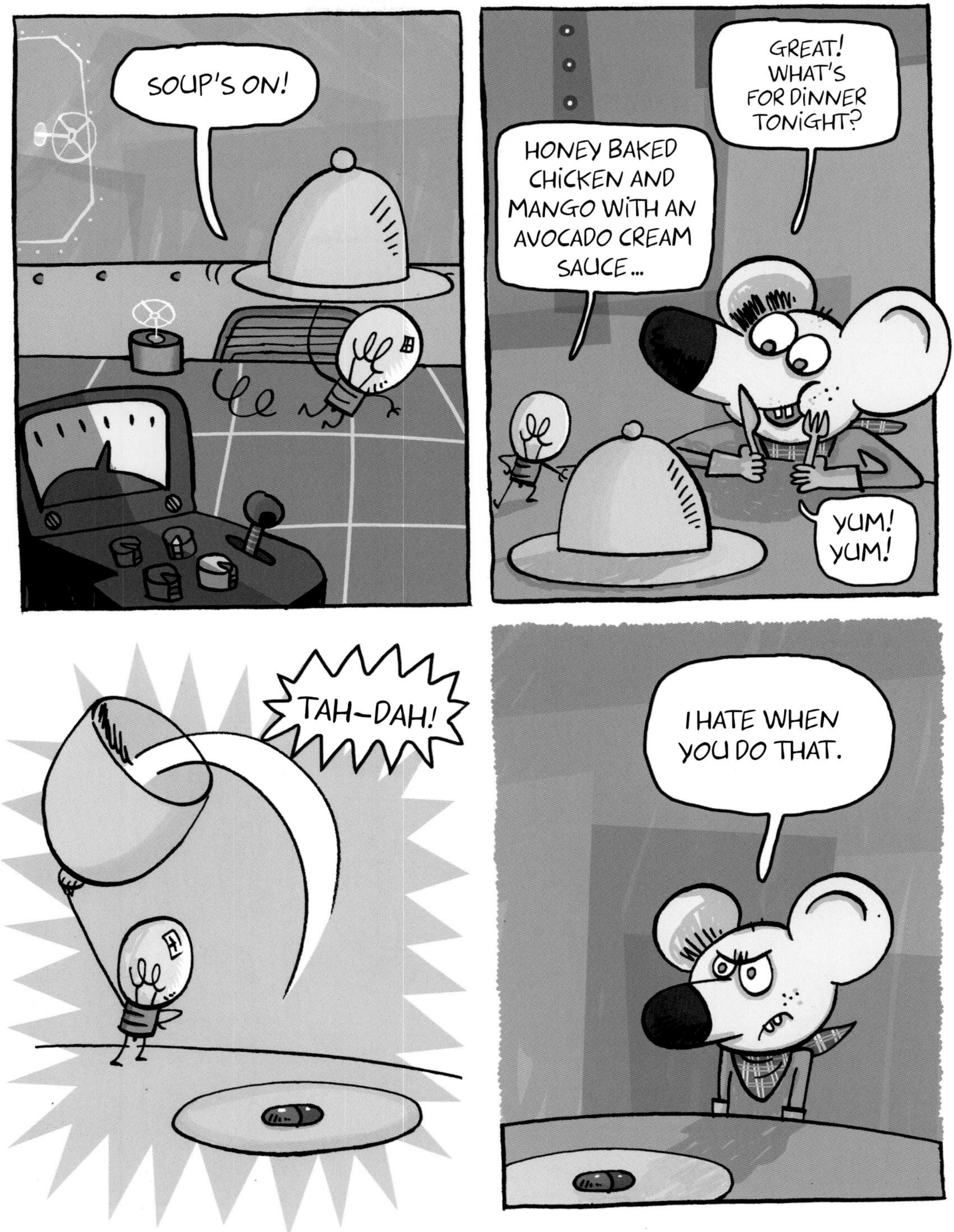
SOUP'S ON!
GREAT! WHAT'S FOR DINNER TONIGHT?
HONEY BAKED CHICKEN AND MANGO WITH AN AVOCADO CREAM SAUCE...
YUM! YUM!
TAH-DAH!
I HATE WHEN YOU DO THAT.

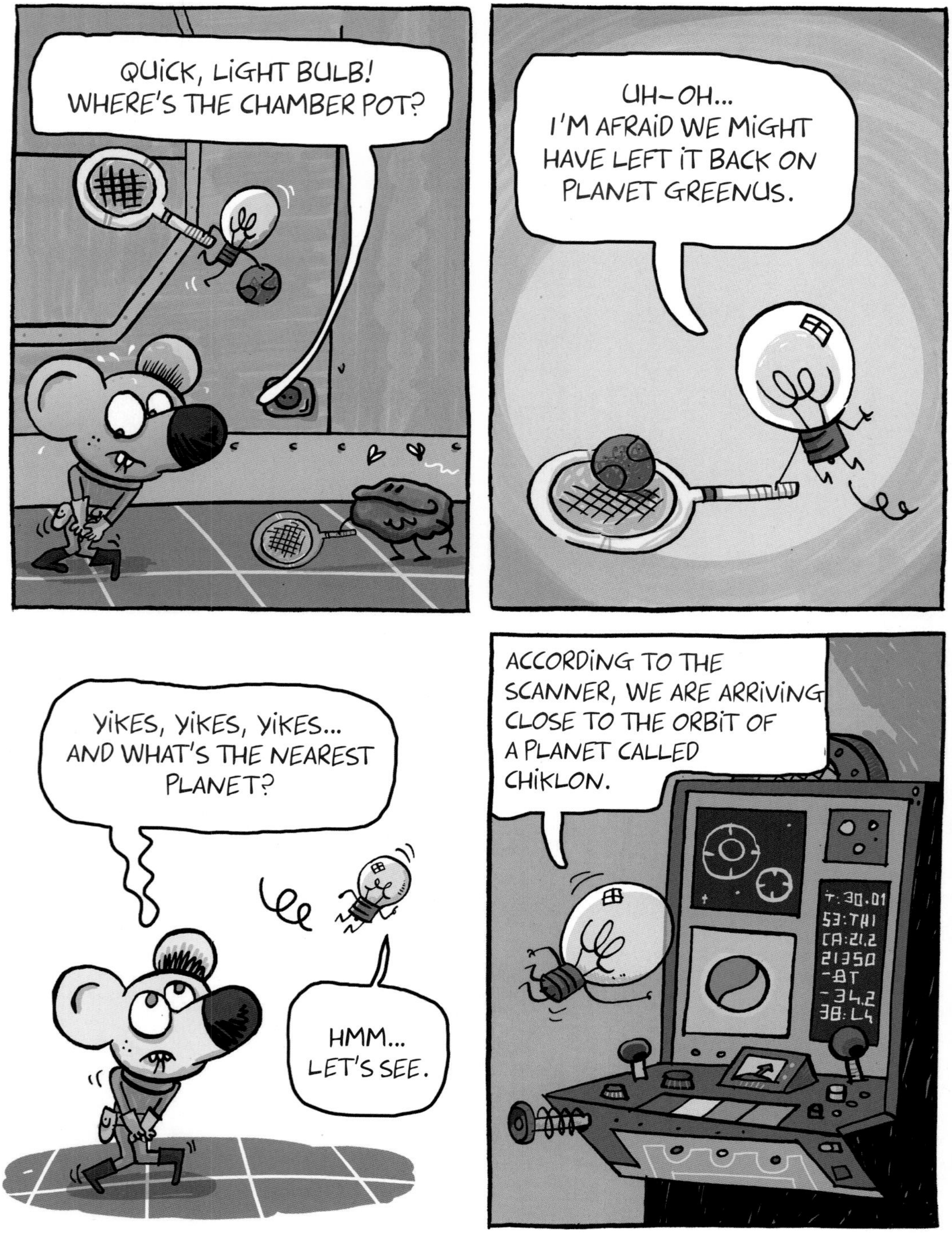
QUICK, LIGHT BULB! WHERE'S THE CHAMBER POT?
UH-OH... I'M AFRAID WE MIGHT HAVE LEFT IT BACK ON PLANET GREENUS.
YIKES, YIKES, YIKES... AND WHAT'S THE NEAREST PLANET?
HMM... LET'S SEE.
ACCORDING TO THE SCANNER, WE ARE ARRIVING CLOSE TO THE ORBIT OF A PLANET CALLED CHIKLON.

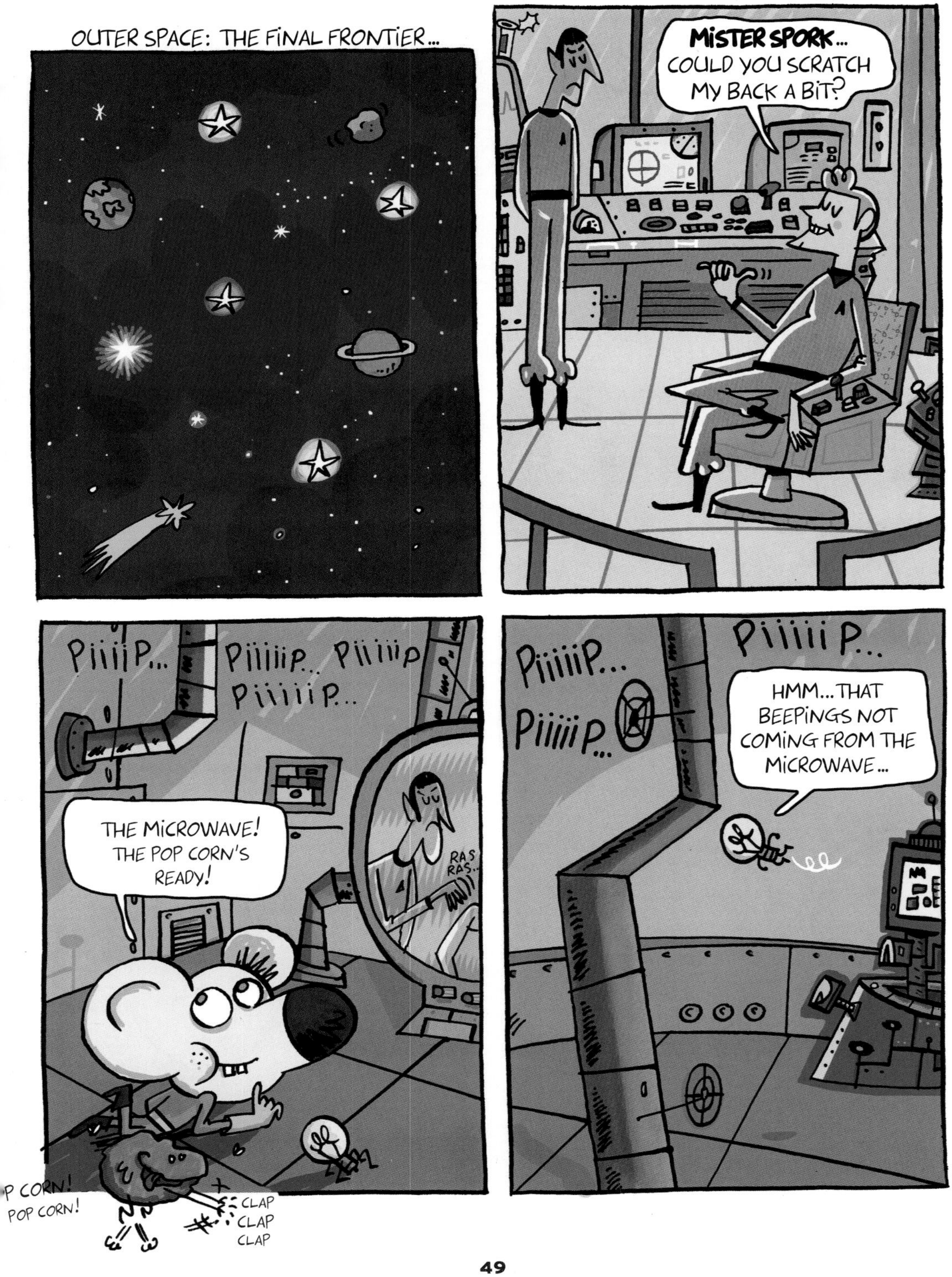
OUTER SPACE: THE FINAL FRONTIER...
MISTER SPORK... COULD YOU SCRATCH MY BACK A BIT?
PiiiiP... Piiiiip... Piiiip Piiiiip...
THE MICROWAVE! THE POP CORN'S READY!
RAS. RAS...
P CORN! POP CORN!
CLAP CLAP CLAP
PiiiiP... PiiiiP... Piiiii P...
HMM... THAT BEEPINGS NOT COMING FROM THE MICROWAVE...

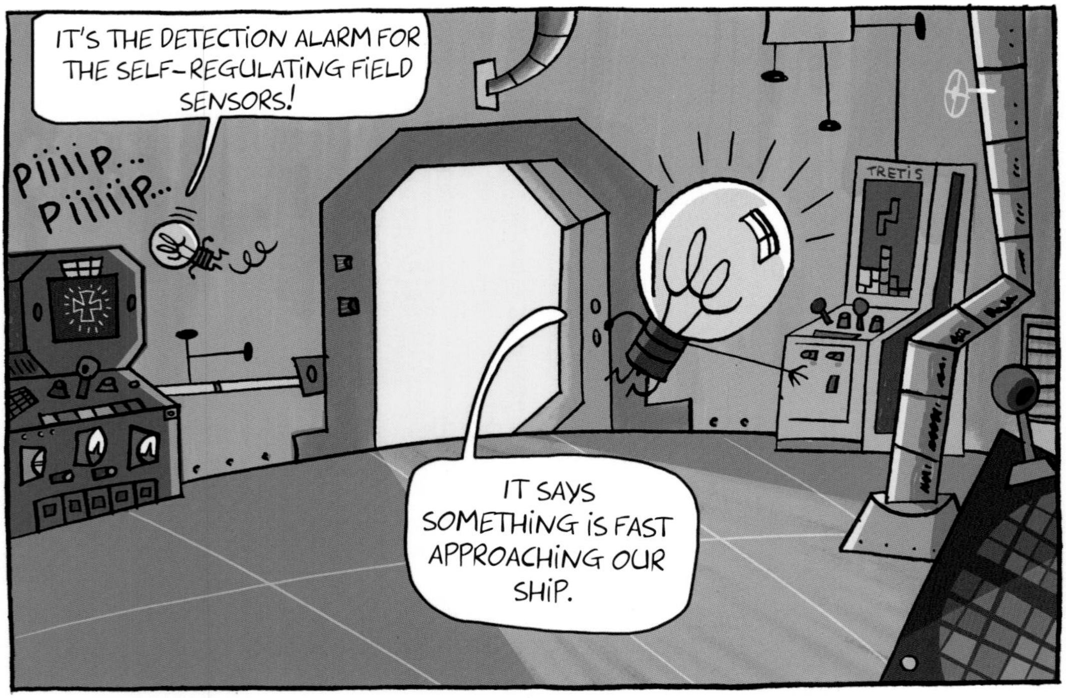
IT'S THE DETECTION ALARM FOR THE SELF-REGULATING FIELD SENSORS!
PIIIIP... PIIIIIP...
TRETIS
IT SAYS SOMETHING IS FAST APPROACHING OUR SHIP.

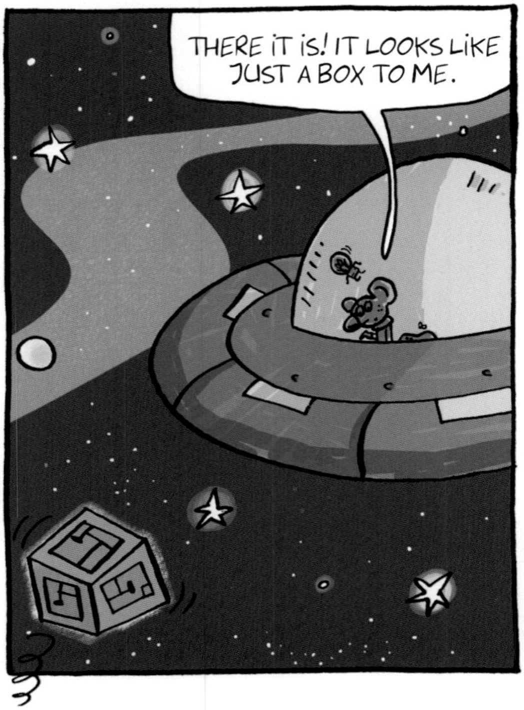
THERE IT IS! IT LOOKS LIKE JUST A BOX TO ME.

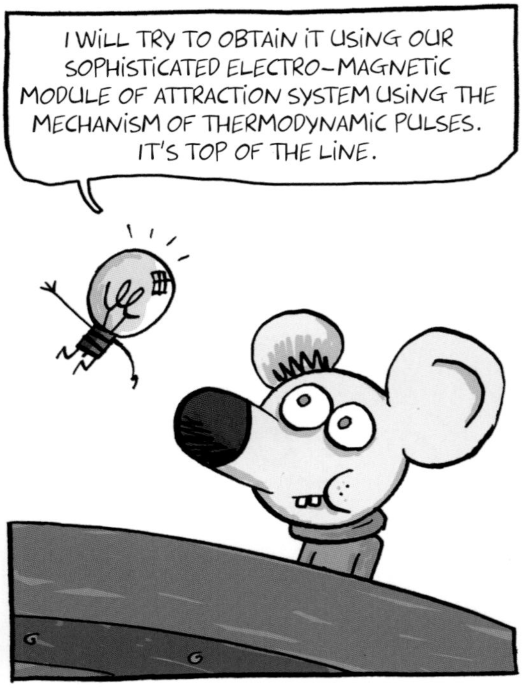
I WILL TRY TO OBTAIN IT USING OUR SOPHISTICATED ELECTRO-MAGNETIC MODULE OF ATTRACTION SYSTEM USING THE MECHANISM OF THERMODYNAMIC PULSES. IT'S TOP OF THE LINE.

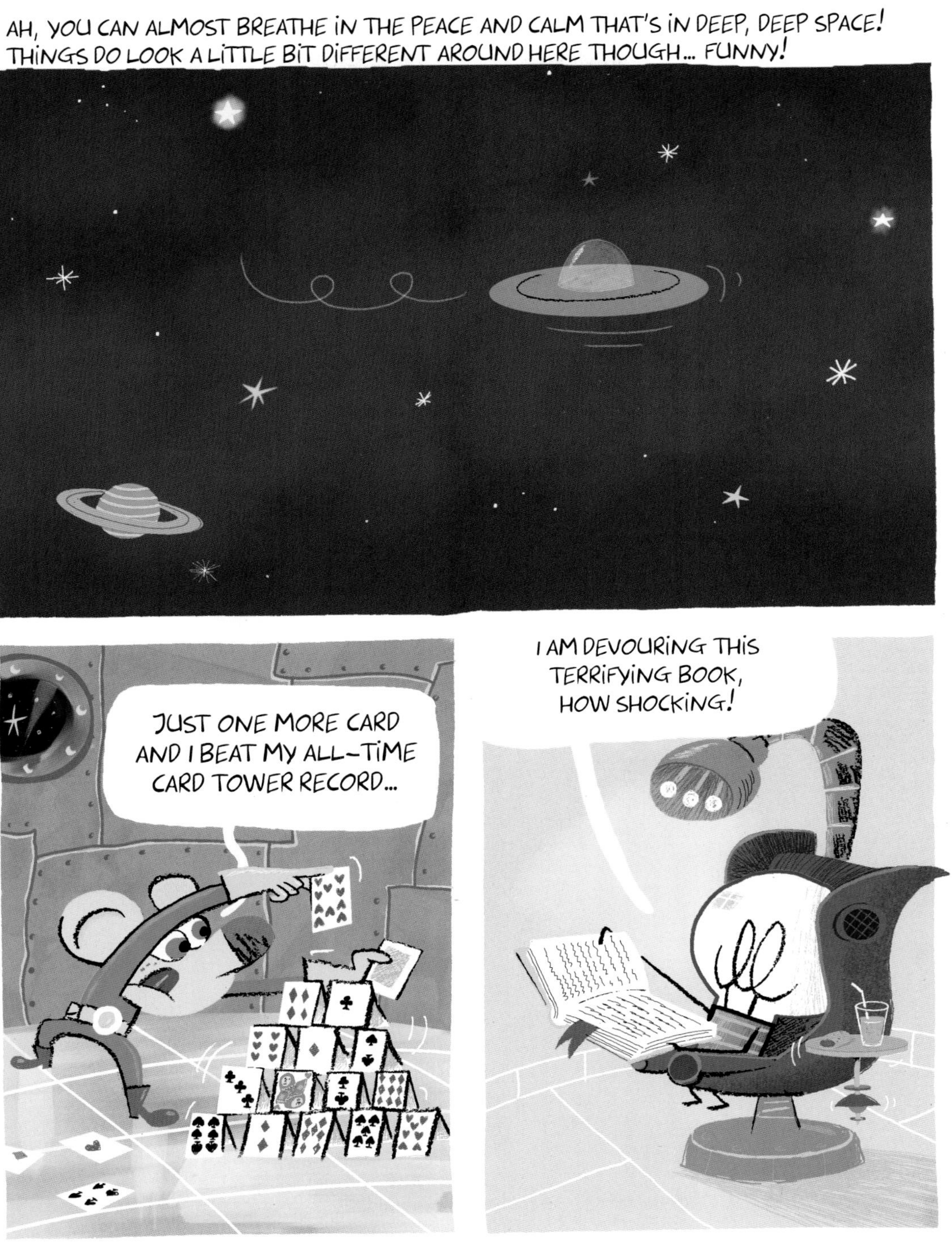
AH, YOU CAN ALMOST BREATHE IN THE PEACE AND CALM THAT'S IN DEEP, DEEP SPACE! THINGS DO LOOK A LITTLE BIT DIFFERENT AROUND HERE THOUGH... FUNNY!
JUST ONE MORE CARD AND I BEAT MY ALL-TIME CARD TOWER RECORD...
I AM DEVOURING THIS TERRIFYING BOOK, HOW SHOCKING!

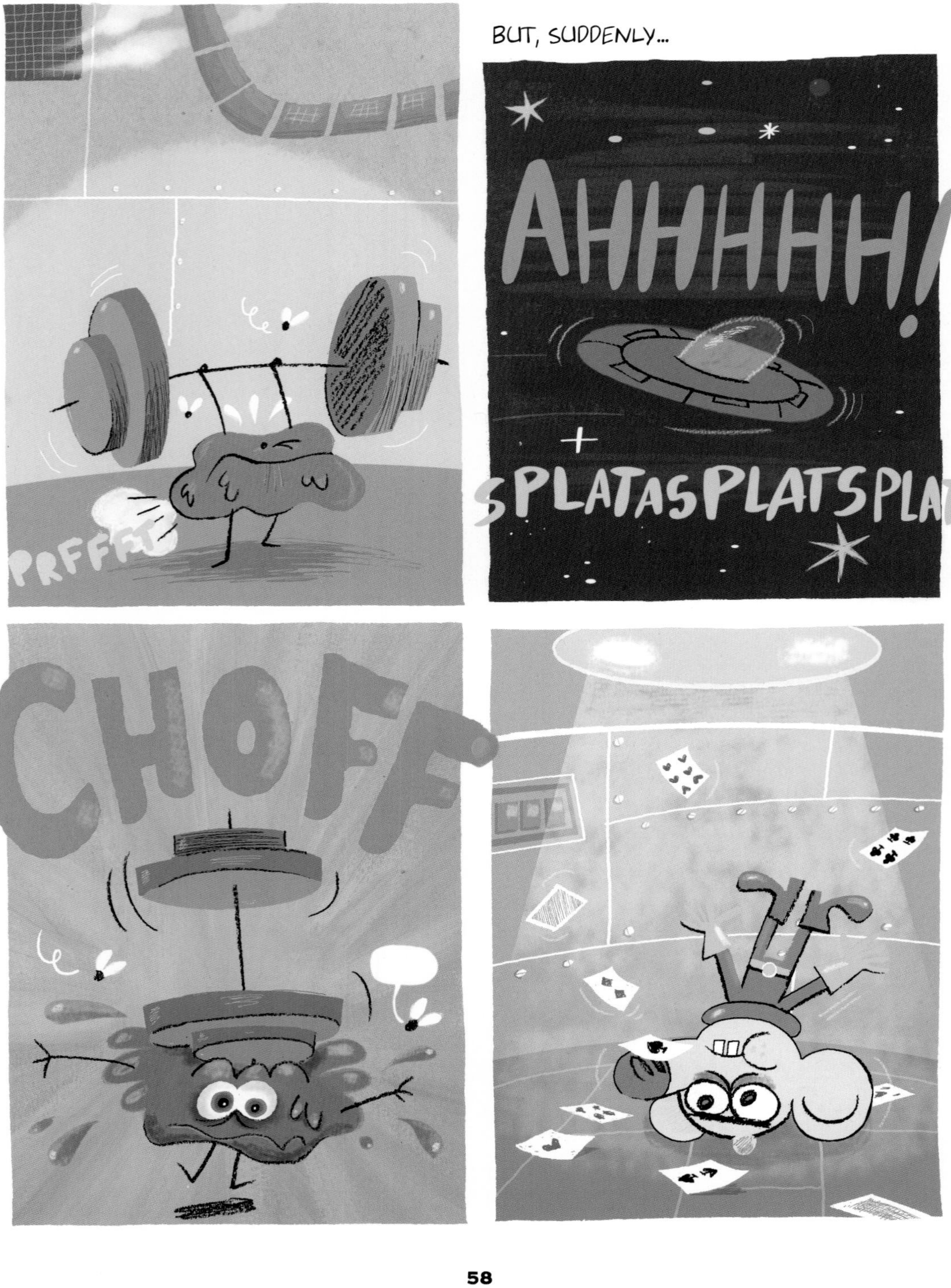
PRFFFT
BUT, SUDDENLY...
AHHHHH!
SPLATASPLATSPLAT
CHOFF

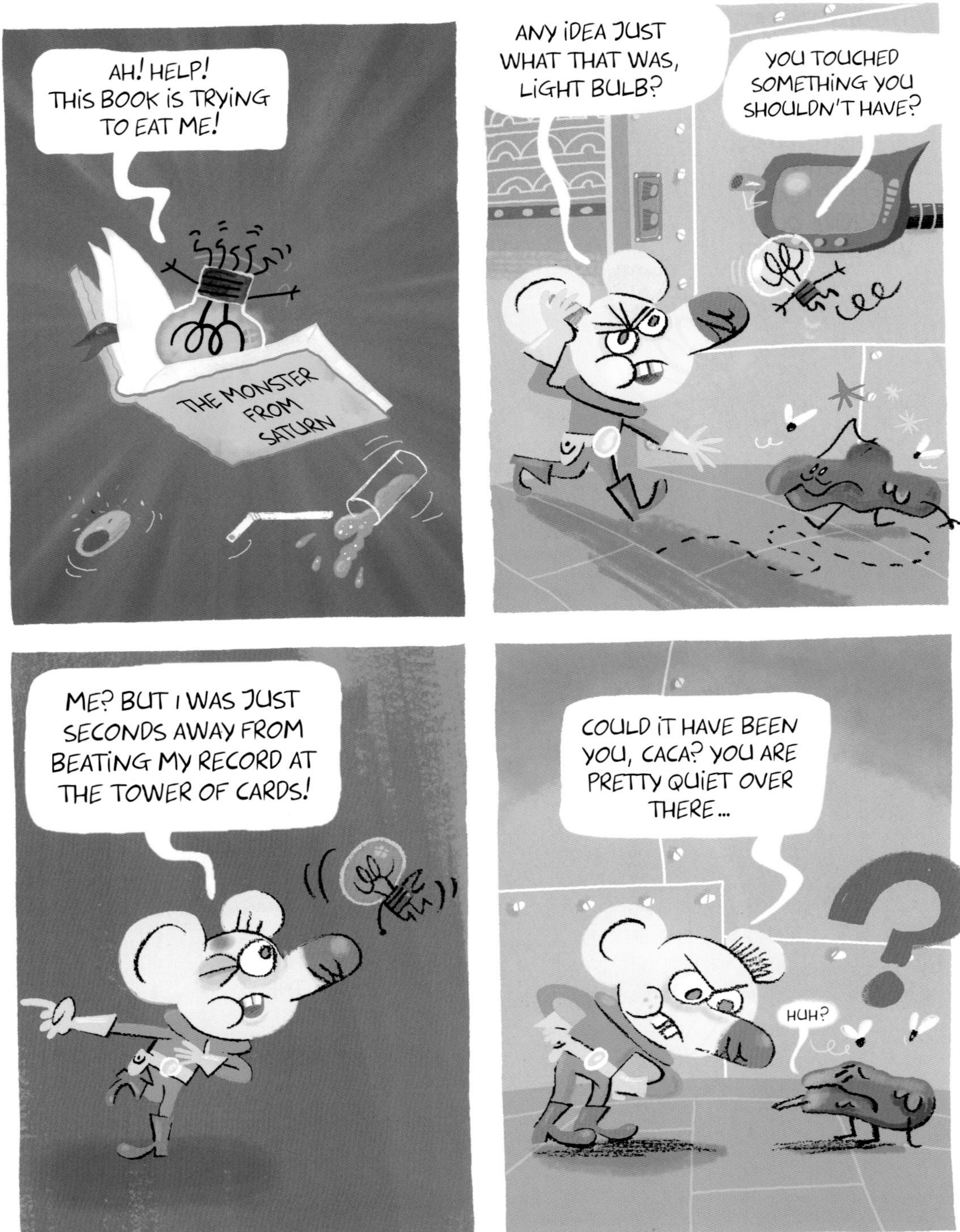
AH! HELP! THIS BOOK IS TRYING TO EAT ME!
THE MONSTER FROM SATURN
ANY IDEA JUST WHAT THAT WAS, LIGHT BULB?
YOU TOUCHED SOMETHING YOU SHOULDN'T HAVE?
ME? BUT I WAS JUST SECONDS AWAY FROM BEATING MY RECORD AT THE TOWER OF CARDS!
COULD IT HAVE BEEN YOU, CACA? YOU ARE PRETTY QUIET OVER THERE...
HUH?

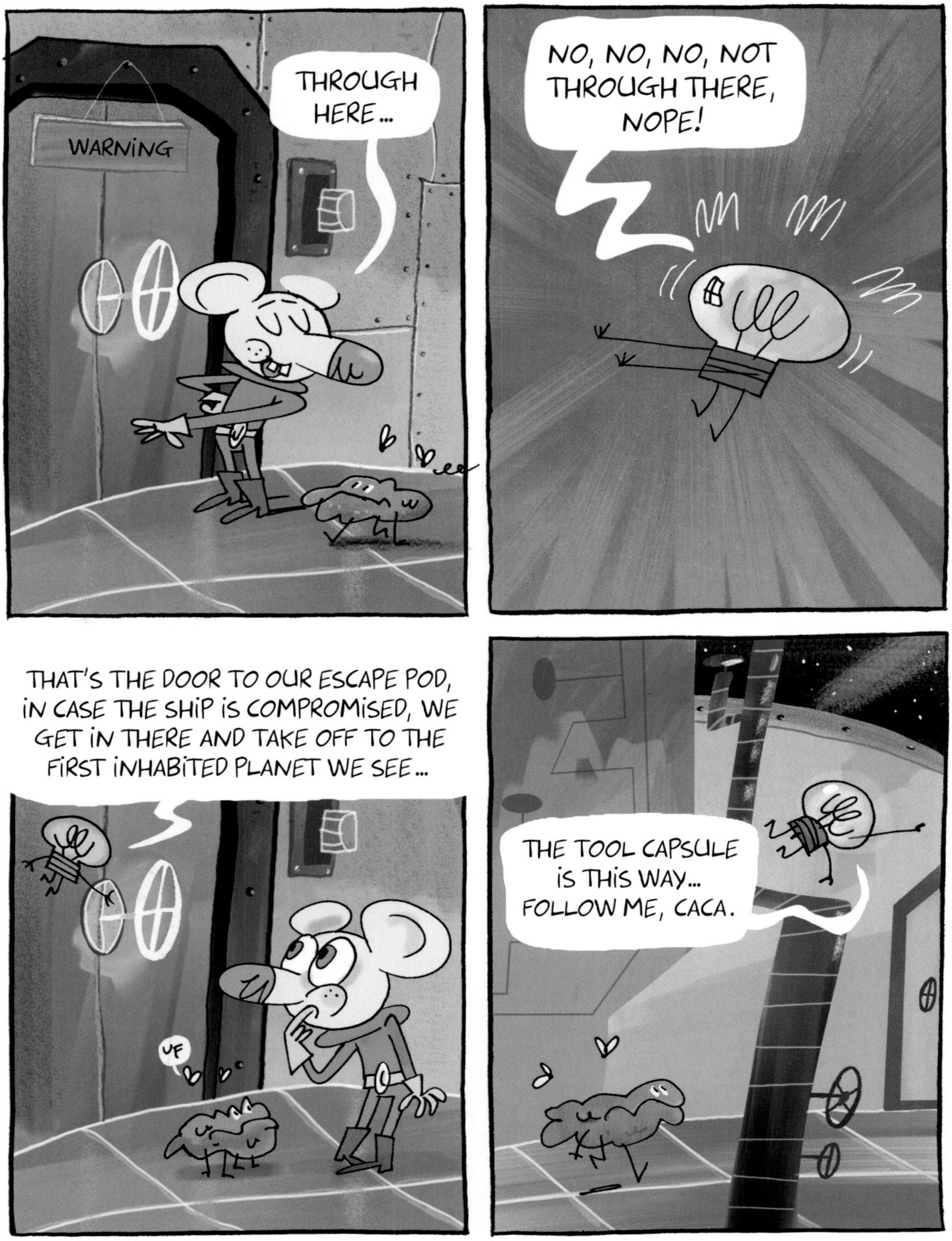
WARNING
THROUGH HERE...
NO, NO, NO, NOT THROUGH THERE, NOPE!
THAT'S THE DOOR TO OUR ESCAPE POD, IN CASE THE SHIP IS COMPROMISED, WE GET IN THERE AND TAKE OFF TO THE FIRST INHABITED PLANET WE SEE...
UF
THE TOOL CAPSULE IS THIS WAY... FOLLOW ME, CACA.

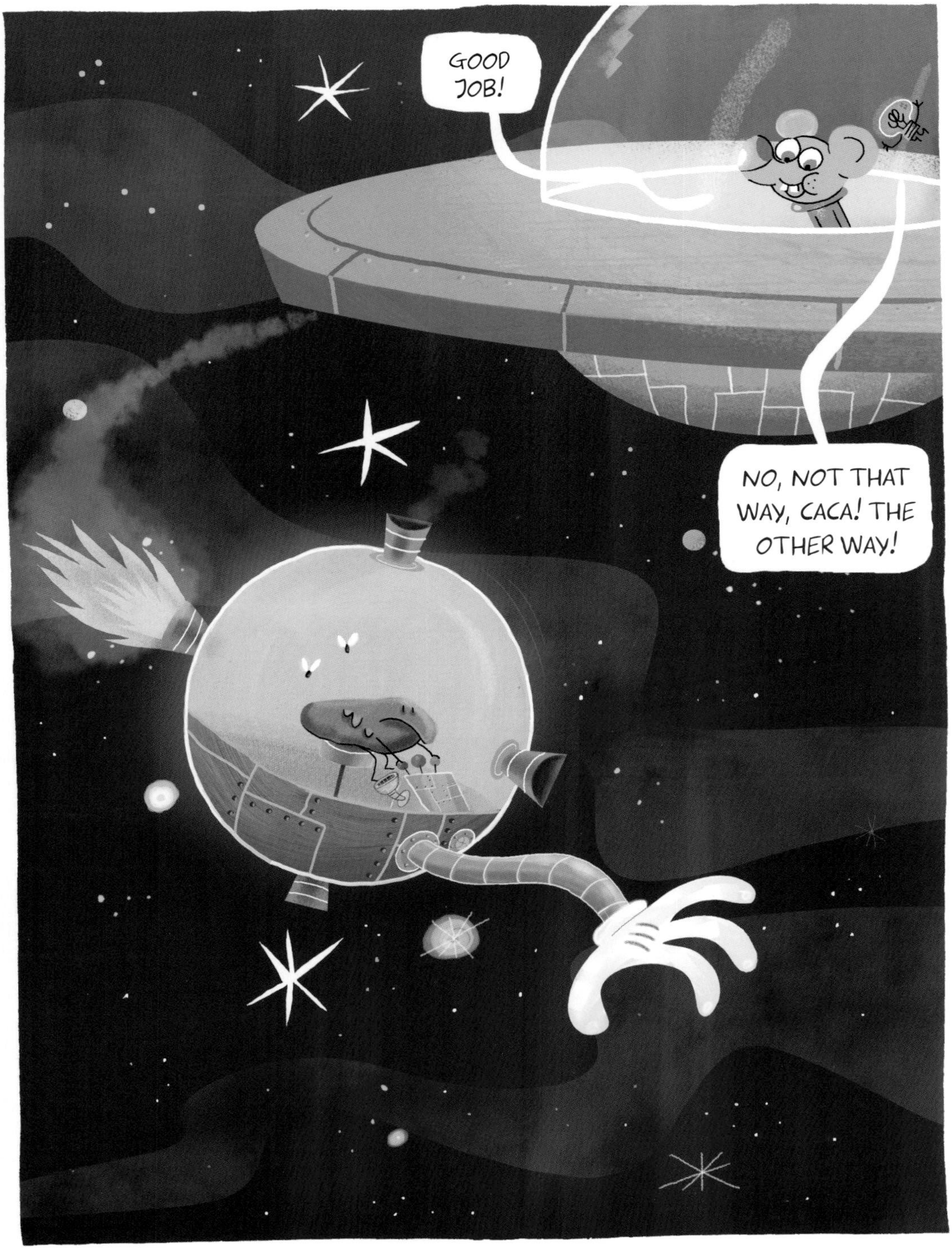
GOOD JOB!
NO, NOT THAT WAY, CACA! THE OTHER WAY!

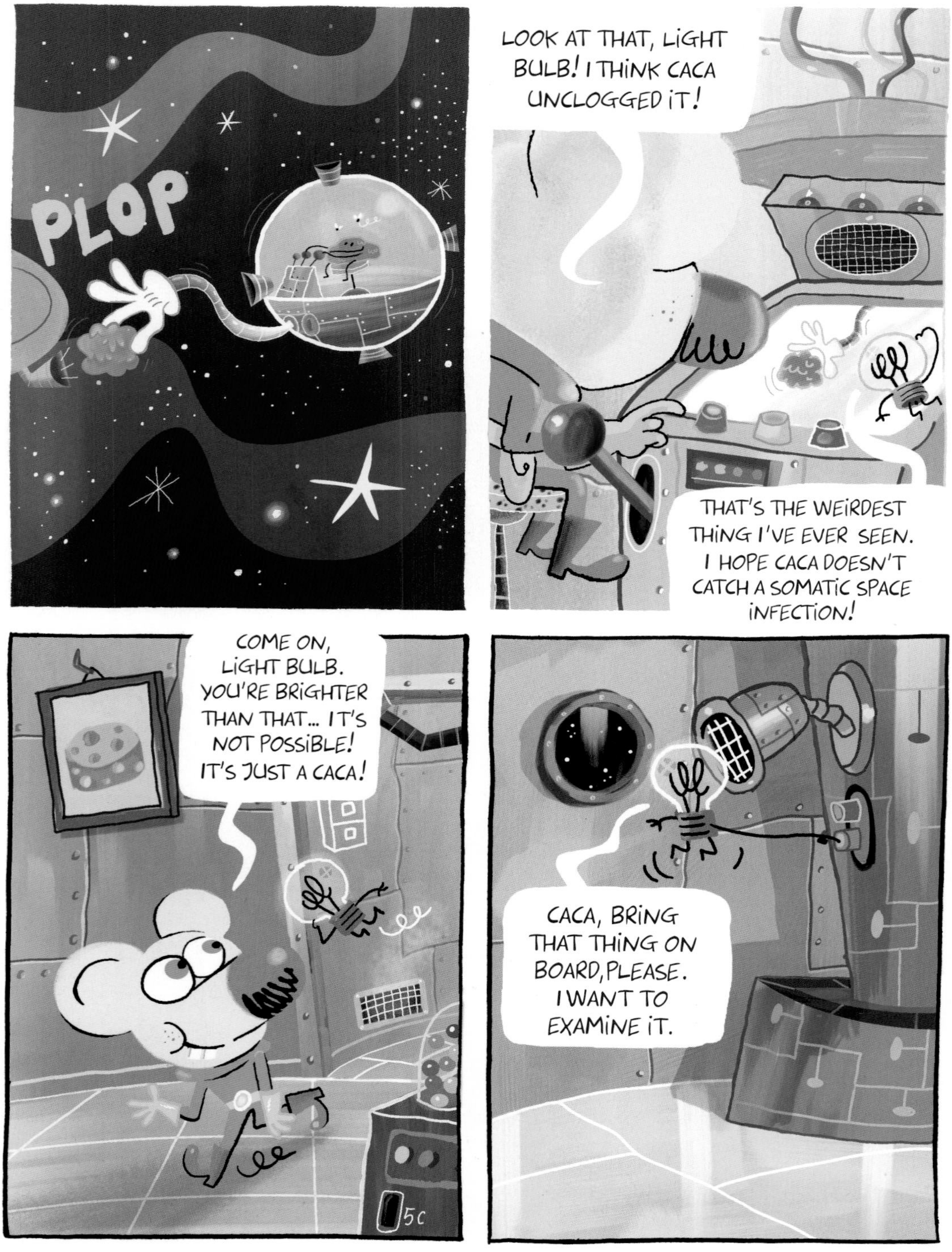
PLOP
LOOK AT THAT, LIGHT BULB! I THINK CACA UNCLOGGED IT!
THAT'S THE WEIRDEST THING I'VE EVER SEEN. I HOPE CACA DOESN'T CATCH A SOMATIC SPACE INFECTION!
COME ON, LIGHT BULB. YOU'RE BRIGHTER THAN THAT... IT'S NOT POSSIBLE! IT'S JUST A CACA!
5C
CACA, BRING THAT THING ON BOARD, PLEASE. I WANT TO EXAMINE IT.

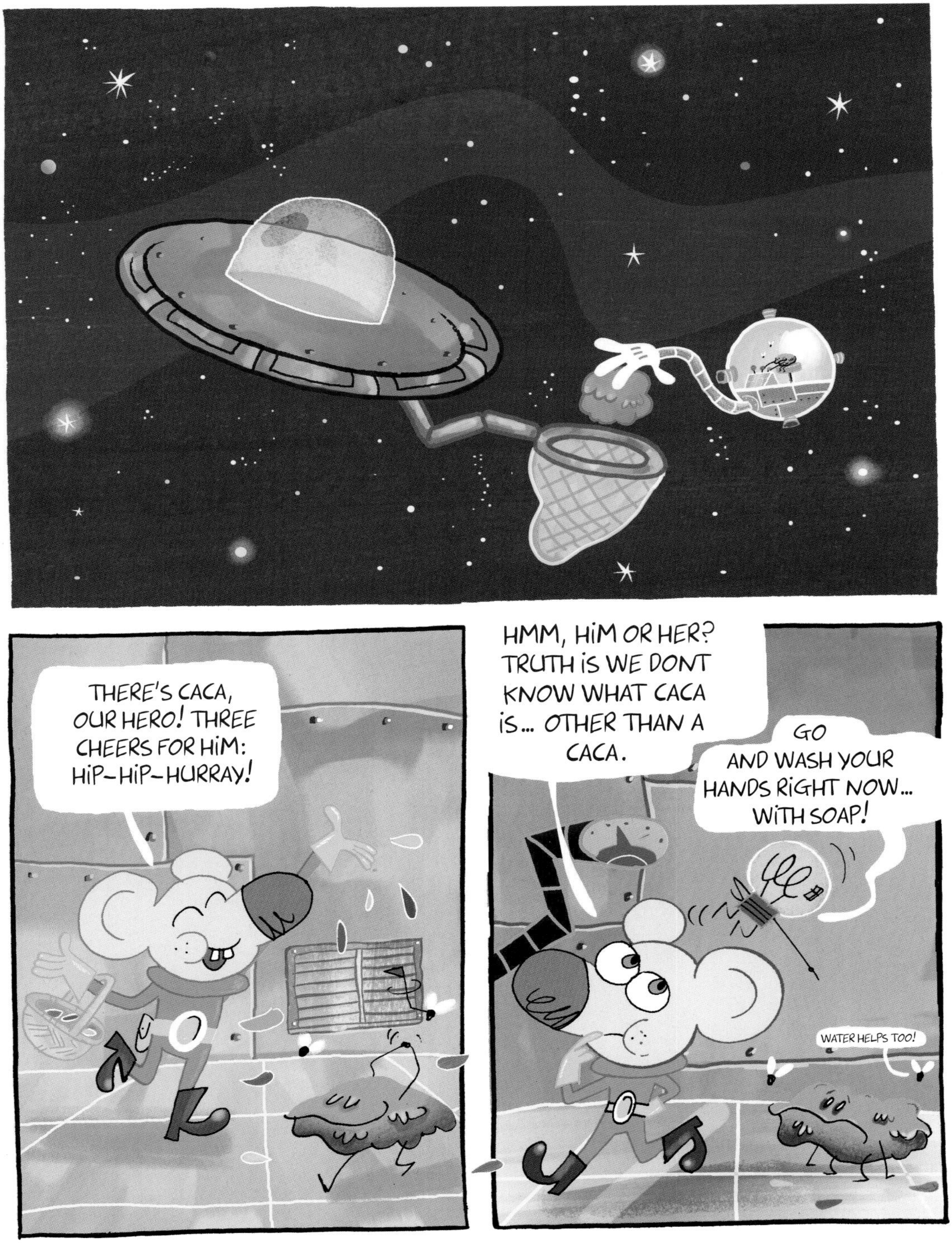
THERE'S CACA, OUR HERO! THREE CHEERS FOR HIM: HIP-HIP-HURRAY!
HMM, HIM OR HER? TRUTH IS WE DONT KNOW WHAT CACA IS... OTHER THAN A CACA.
GO AND WASH YOUR HANDS RIGHT NOW... WITH SOAP!
WATER HELPS TOO!

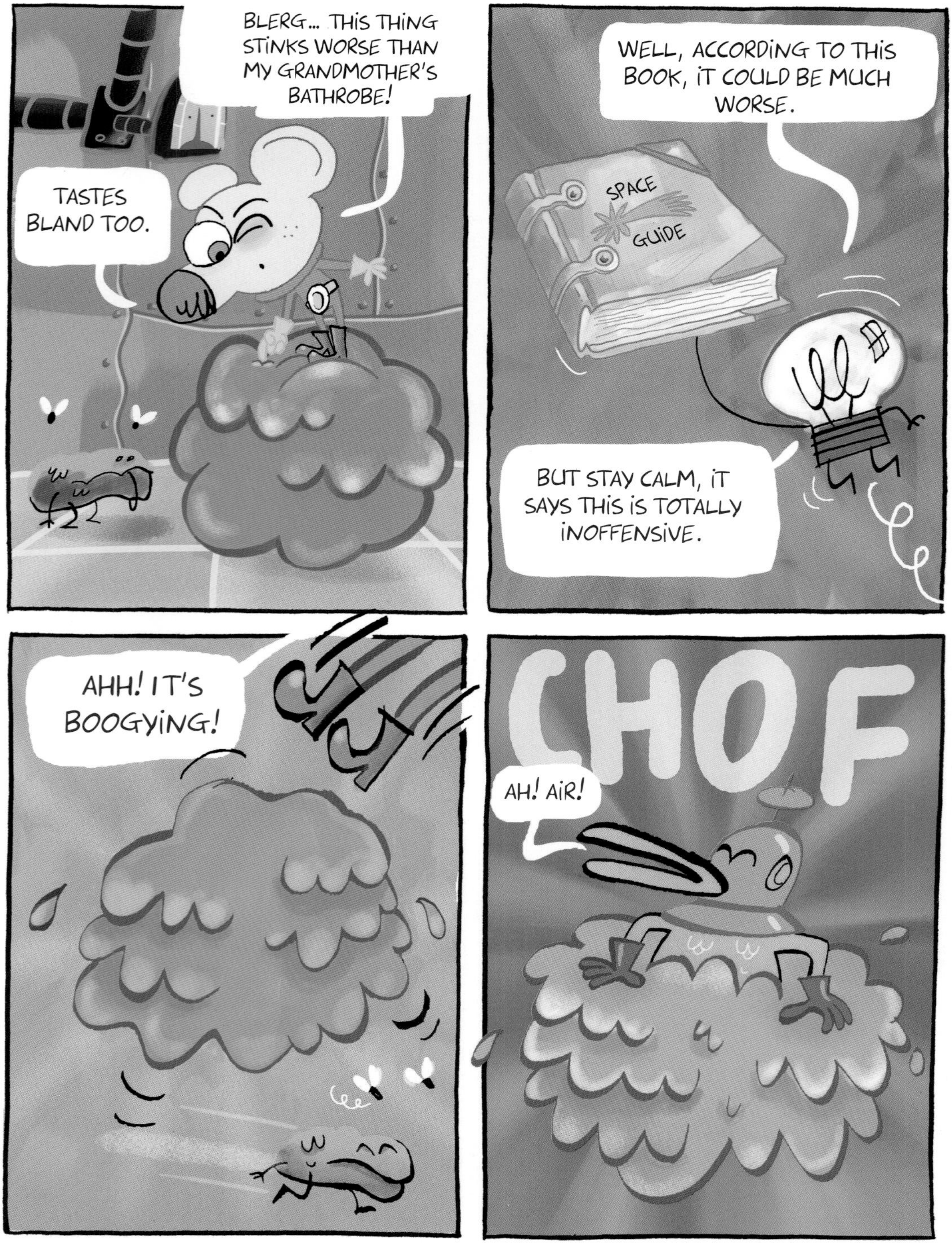
BLERG... THIS THING STINKS WORSE THAN MY GRANDMOTHER'S BATHROBE!
TASTES BLAND TOO.
WELL, ACCORDING TO THIS BOOK, IT COULD BE MUCH WORSE.
SPACE GUIDE
BUT STAY CALM, IT SAYS THIS IS TOTALLY INOFFENSIVE.
AHH! IT'S BOOGYING!
CHOF
AH! AIR!

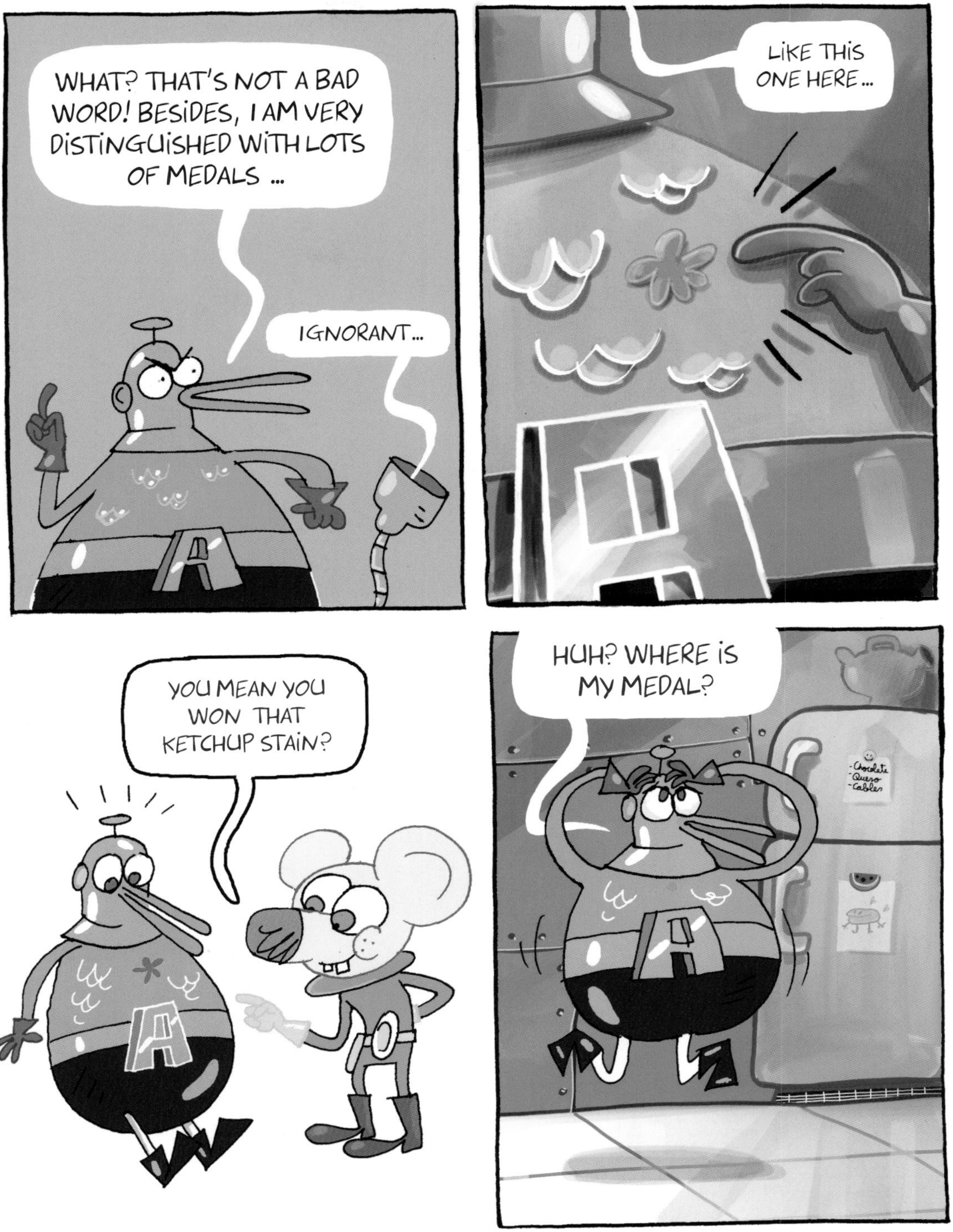
WHAT? THAT'S NOT A BAD WORD! BESIDES, I AM VERY DISTINGUISHED WITH LOTS OF MEDALS ...
IGNORANT...
LIKE THIS ONE HERE...
YOU MEAN YOU WON THAT KETCHUP STAIN?
HUH? WHERE IS MY MEDAL?
-Chocolate
-Queso
-Cables

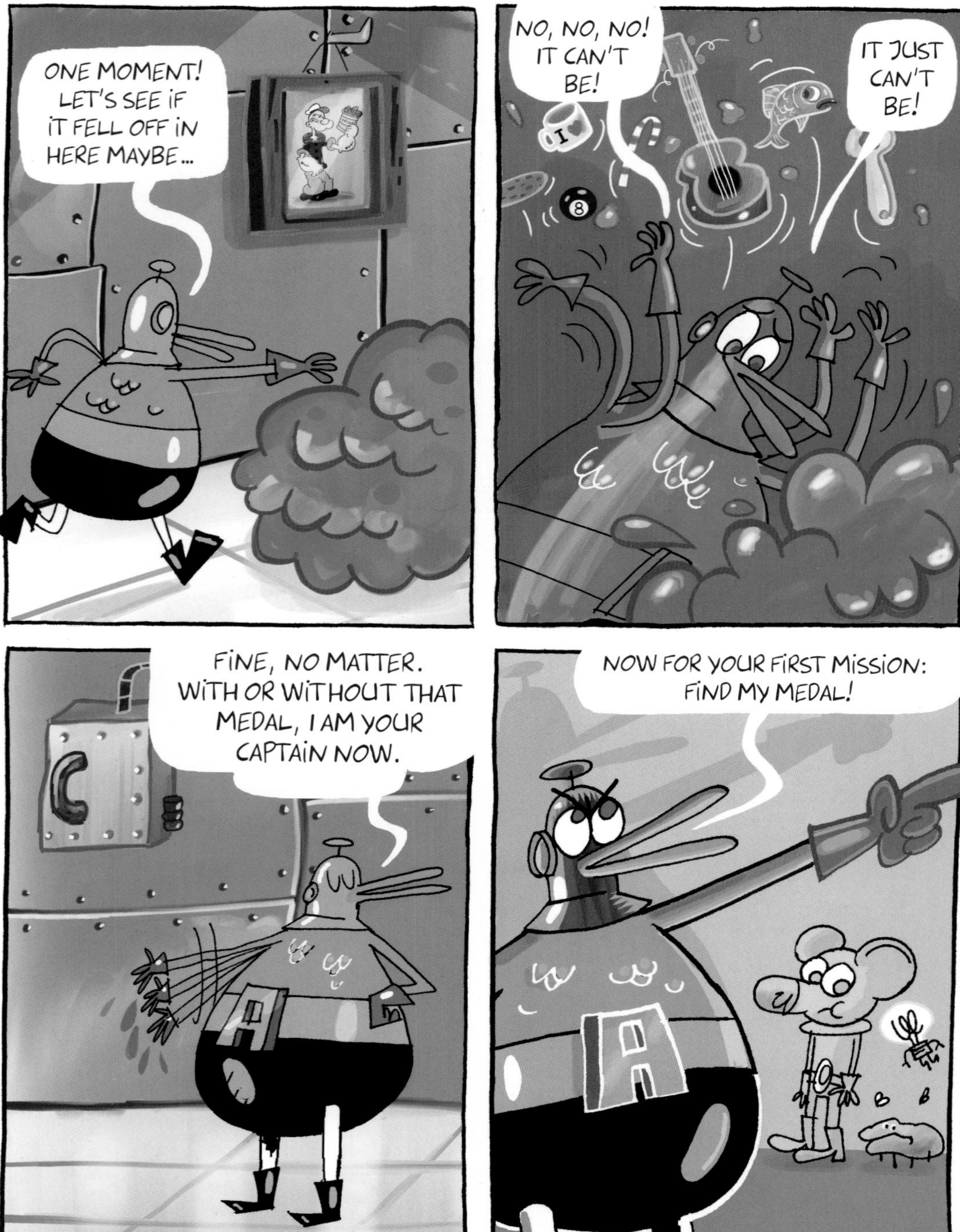
ONE MOMENT! LET'S SEE IF IT FELL OFF IN HERE MAYBE...
NO, NO, NO! IT CAN'T BE!
IT JUST CAN'T BE!
I
8
FINE, NO MATTER. WITH OR WITHOUT THAT MEDAL, I AM YOUR CAPTAIN NOW.
A
NOW FOR YOUR FIRST MISSION: FIND MY MEDAL!
A

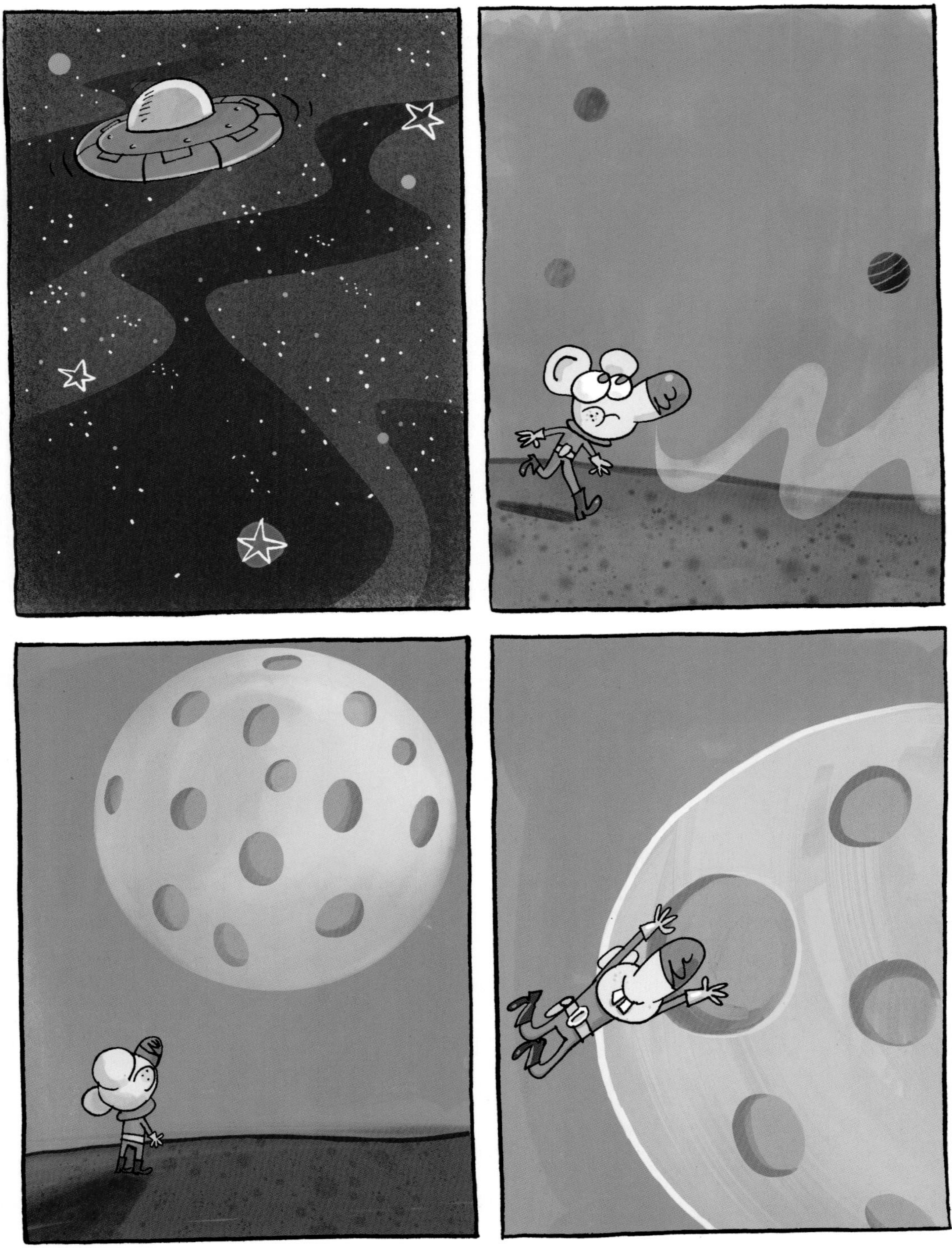

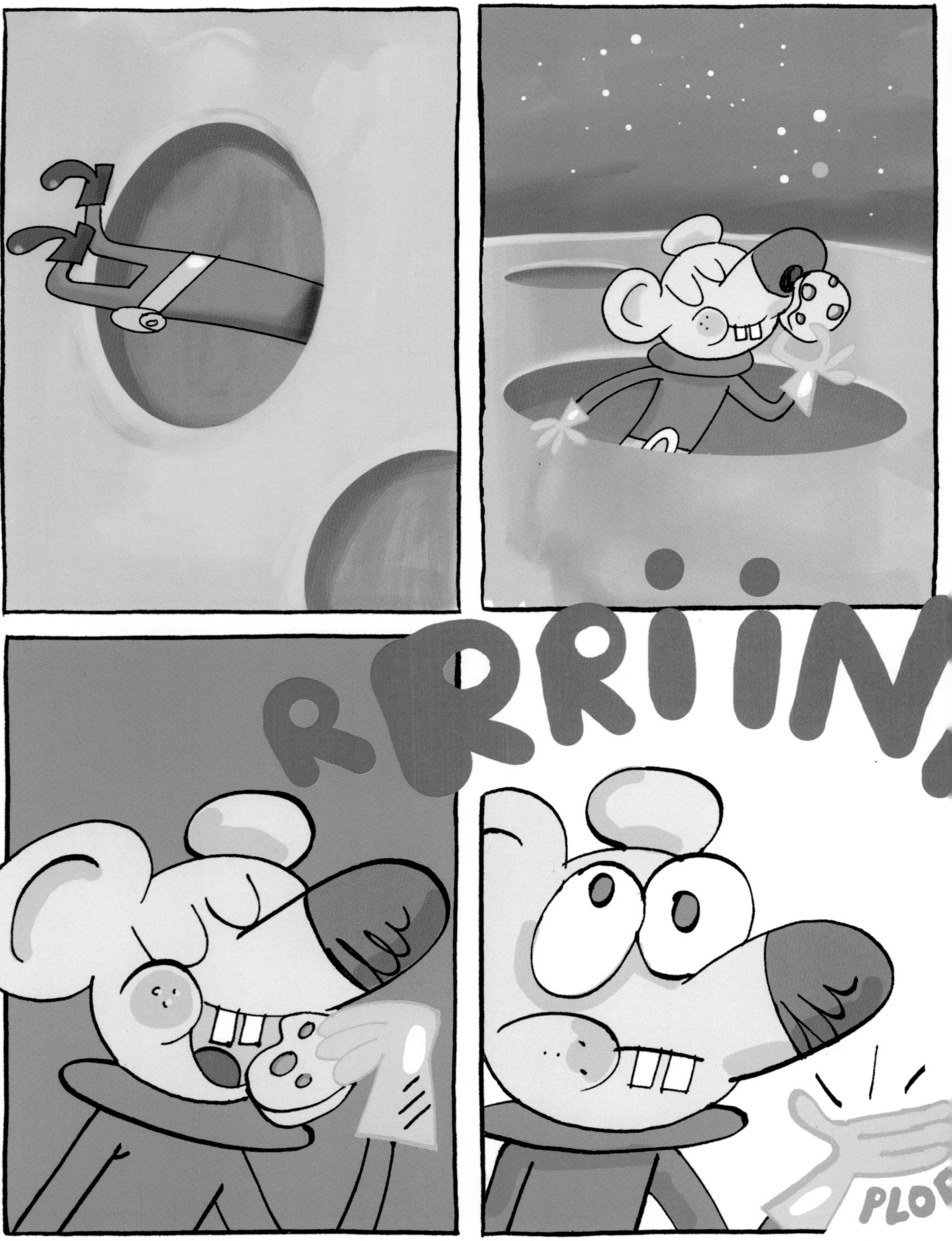
RRRIIN
PLO

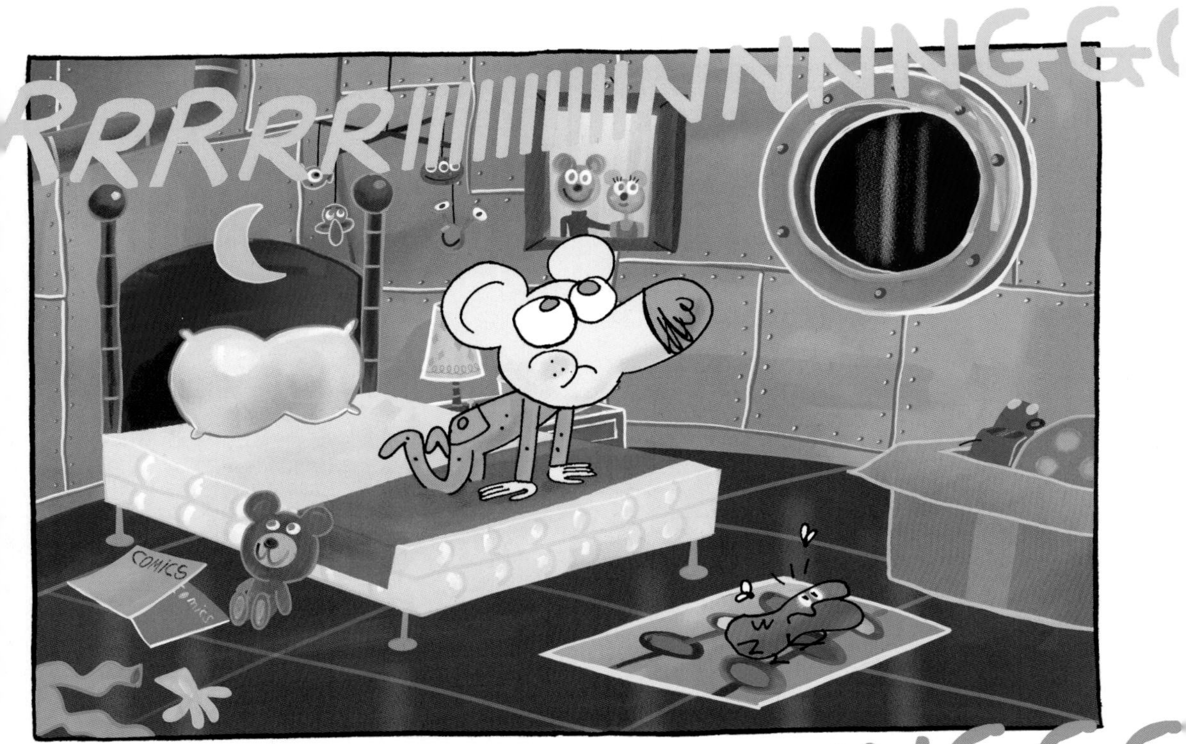
RRRRRIIIIIIIIIIIIIIIIINNNNNGG
COMICS

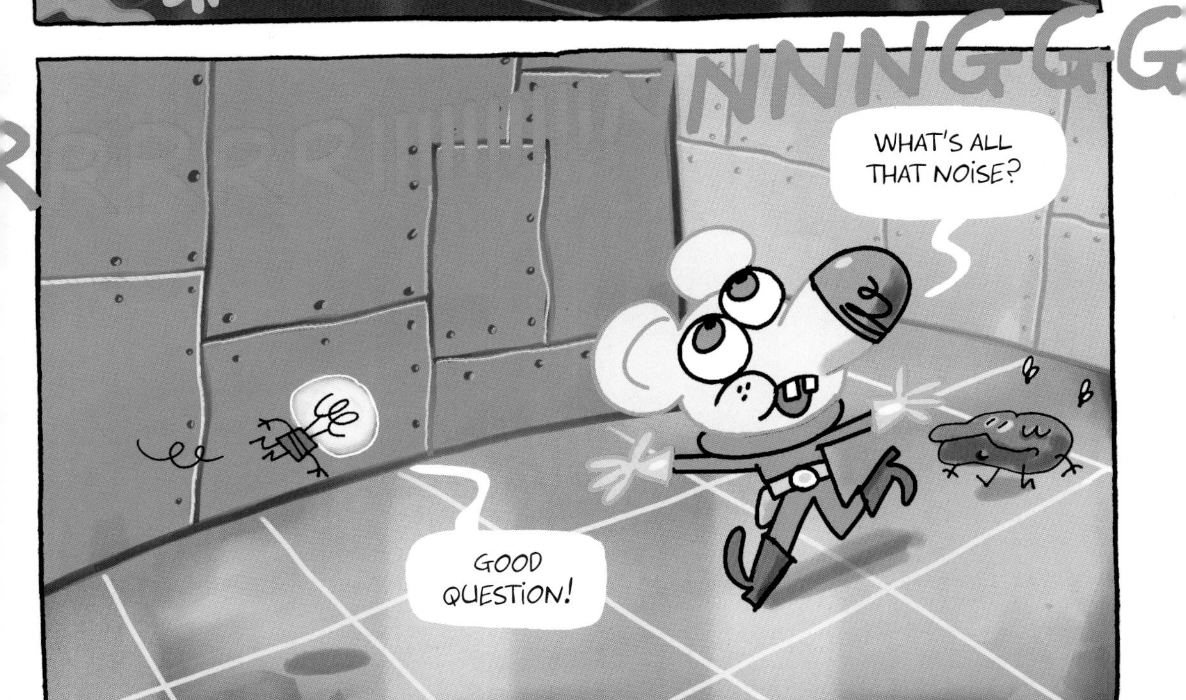
RRRRRIIIIIIIIIIINNNNNGGG
WHAT'S ALL THAT NOISE?
GOOD QUESTION!

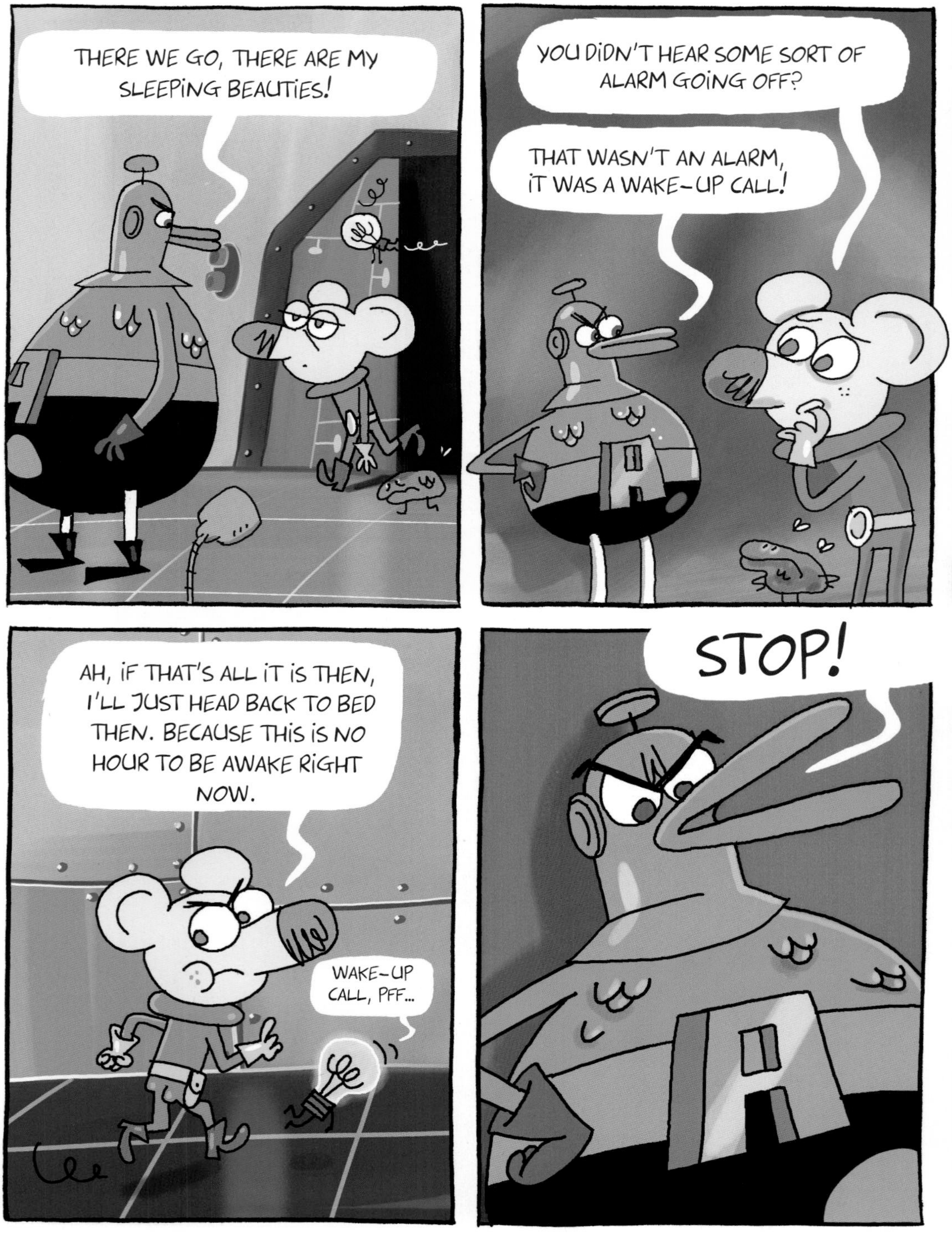
THERE WE GO, THERE ARE MY SLEEPING BEAUTIES!
YOU DIDN'T HEAR SOME SORT OF ALARM GOING OFF?
THAT WASN'T AN ALARM, IT WAS A WAKE-UP CALL!
AH, IF THAT'S ALL IT IS THEN, I'LL JUST HEAD BACK TO BED THEN. BECAUSE THIS IS NO HOUR TO BE AWAKE RIGHT NOW.
WAKE-UP CALL, PFF...
STOP!

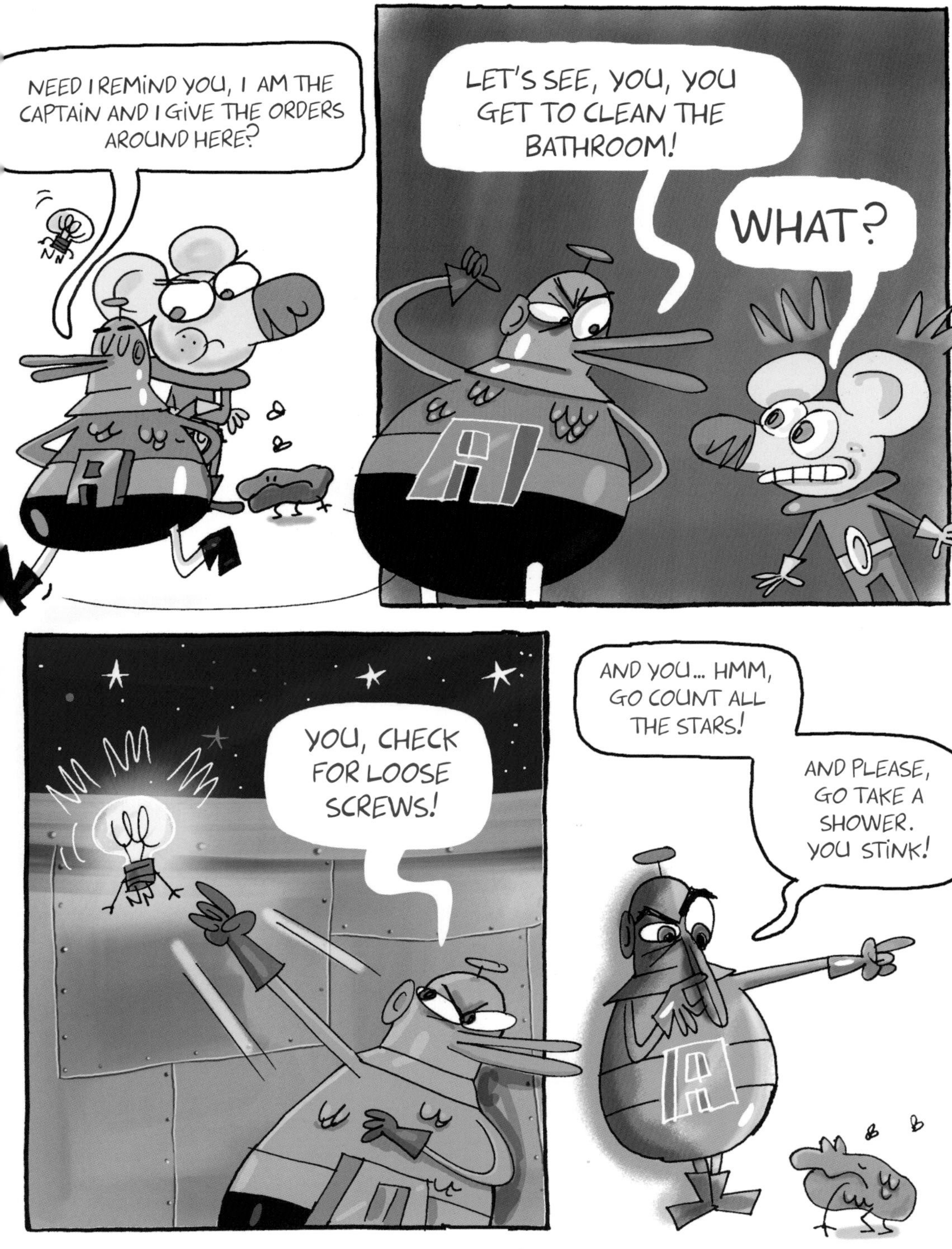
NEED I REMIND YOU, I AM THE CAPTAIN AND I GIVE THE ORDERS AROUND HERE?
LET'S SEE, YOU, YOU GET TO CLEAN THE BATHROOM!
WHAT?
YOU, CHECK FOR LOOSE SCREWS!
AND YOU... HMM, GO COUNT ALL THE STARS!
AND PLEASE, GO TAKE A SHOWER. YOU STINK!

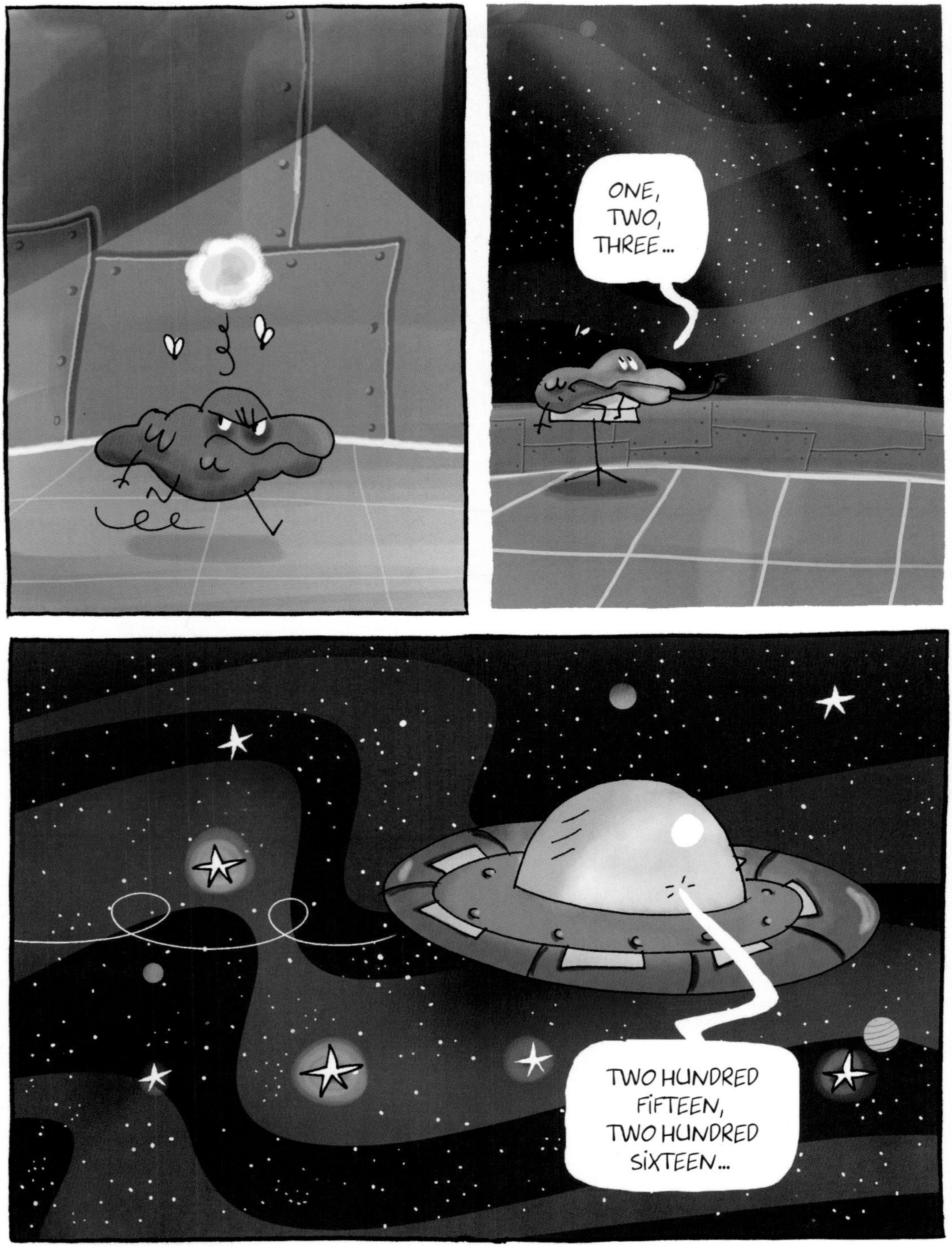
ONE, TWO, THREE...
TWO HUNDRED FIFTEEN, TWO HUNDRED SIXTEEN...

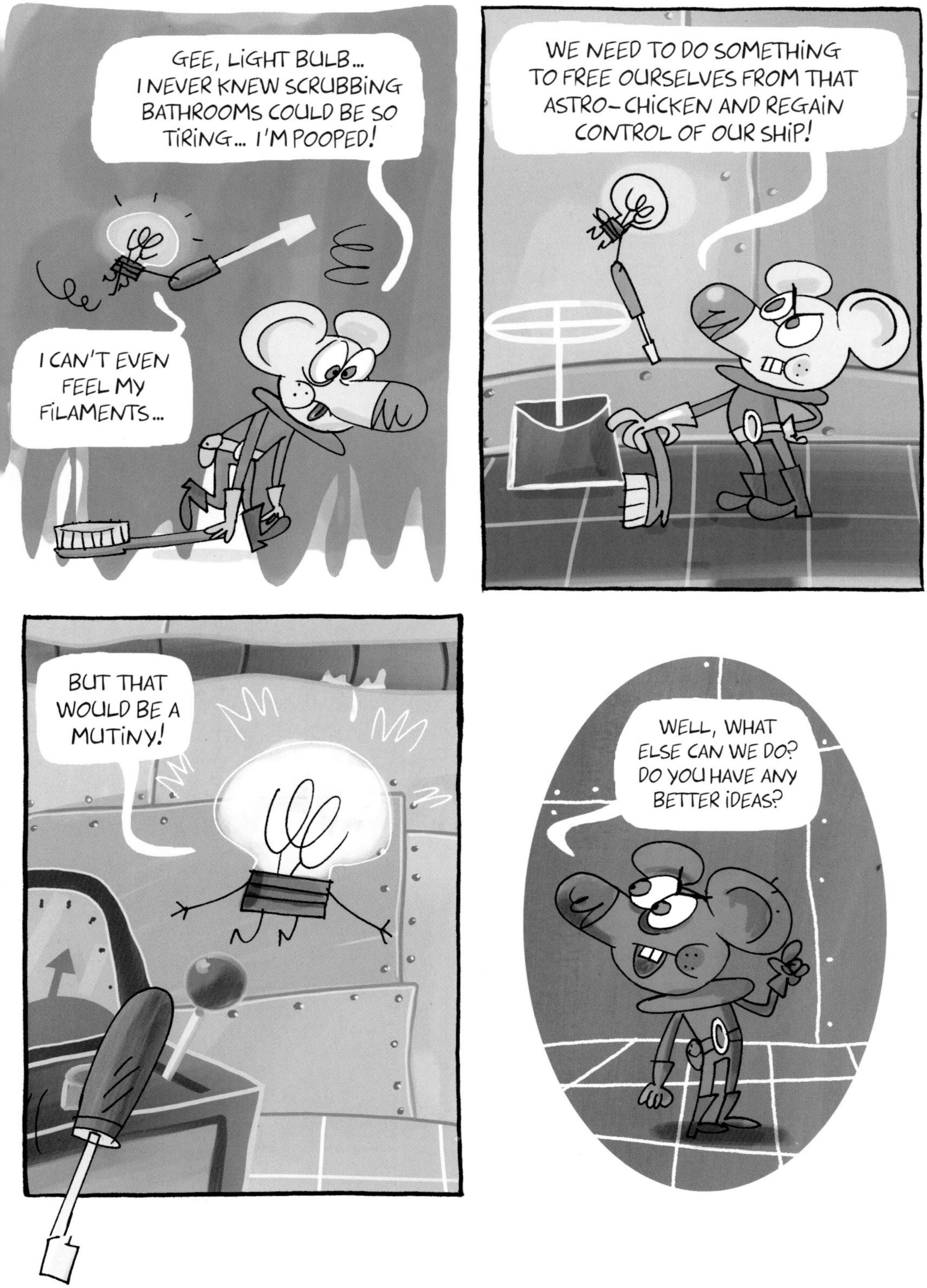
GEE, LIGHT BULB... I NEVER KNEW SCRUBBING BATHROOMS COULD BE SO TIRING... I'M POOPED!
I CAN'T EVEN FEEL MY FILAMENTS...
WE NEED TO DO SOMETHING TO FREE OURSELVES FROM THAT ASTRO-CHICKEN AND REGAIN CONTROL OF OUR SHIP!
BUT THAT WOULD BE A MUTINY!
WELL, WHAT ELSE CAN WE DO? DO YOU HAVE ANY BETTER IDEAS?

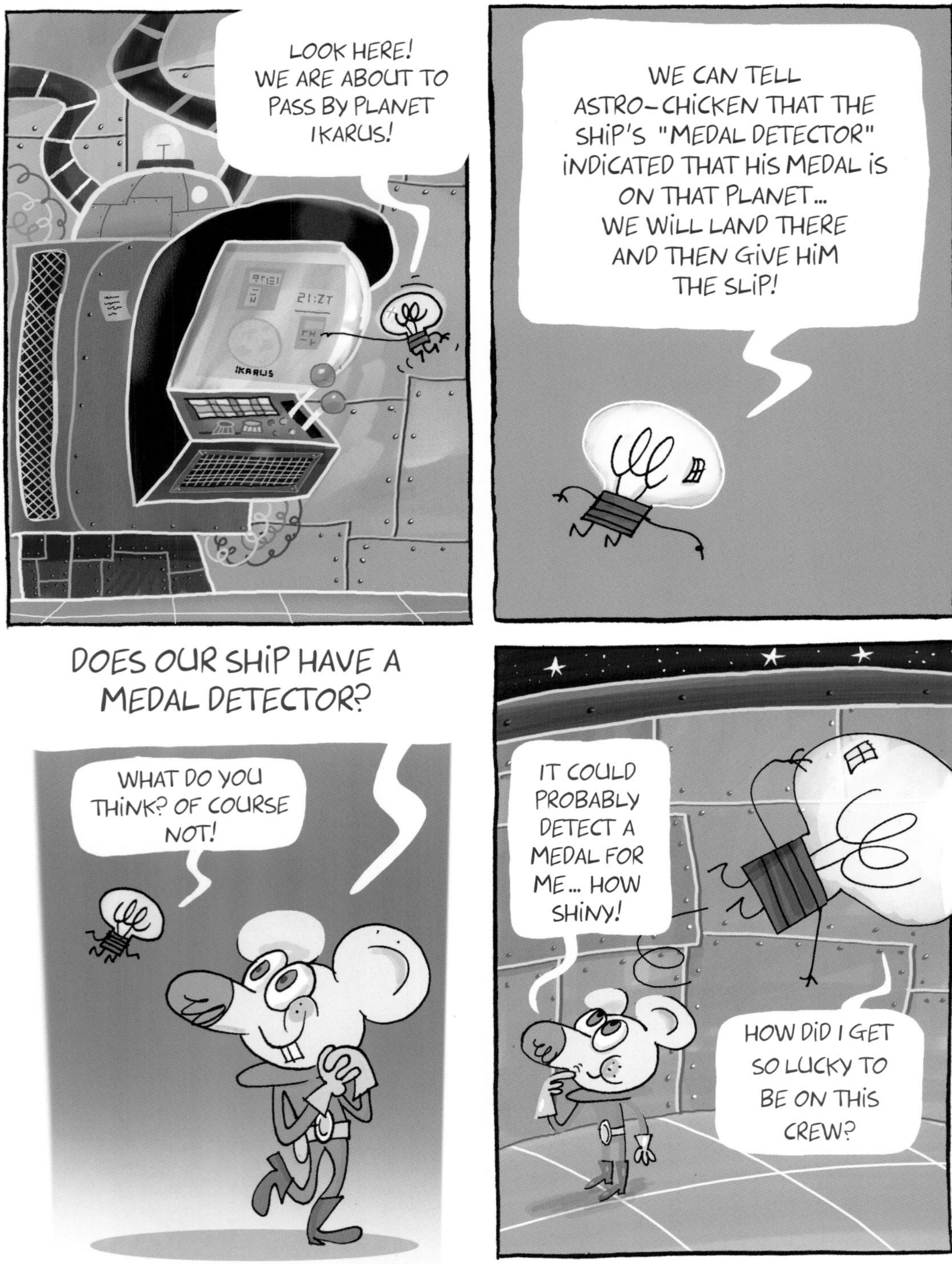
LOOK HERE! WE ARE ABOUT TO PASS BY PLANET IKARUS!
IKARUS
21:ZT
WE CAN TELL ASTRO-CHICKEN THAT THE SHIP'S "MEDAL DETECTOR" INDICATED THAT HIS MEDAL IS ON THAT PLANET... WE WILL LAND THERE AND THEN GIVE HIM THE SLIP!
DOES OUR SHIP HAVE A MEDAL DETECTOR?
WHAT DO YOU THINK? OF COURSE NOT!
IT COULD PROBABLY DETECT A MEDAL FOR ME... HOW SHINY!
HOW DID I GET SO LUCKY TO BE ON THIS CREW?

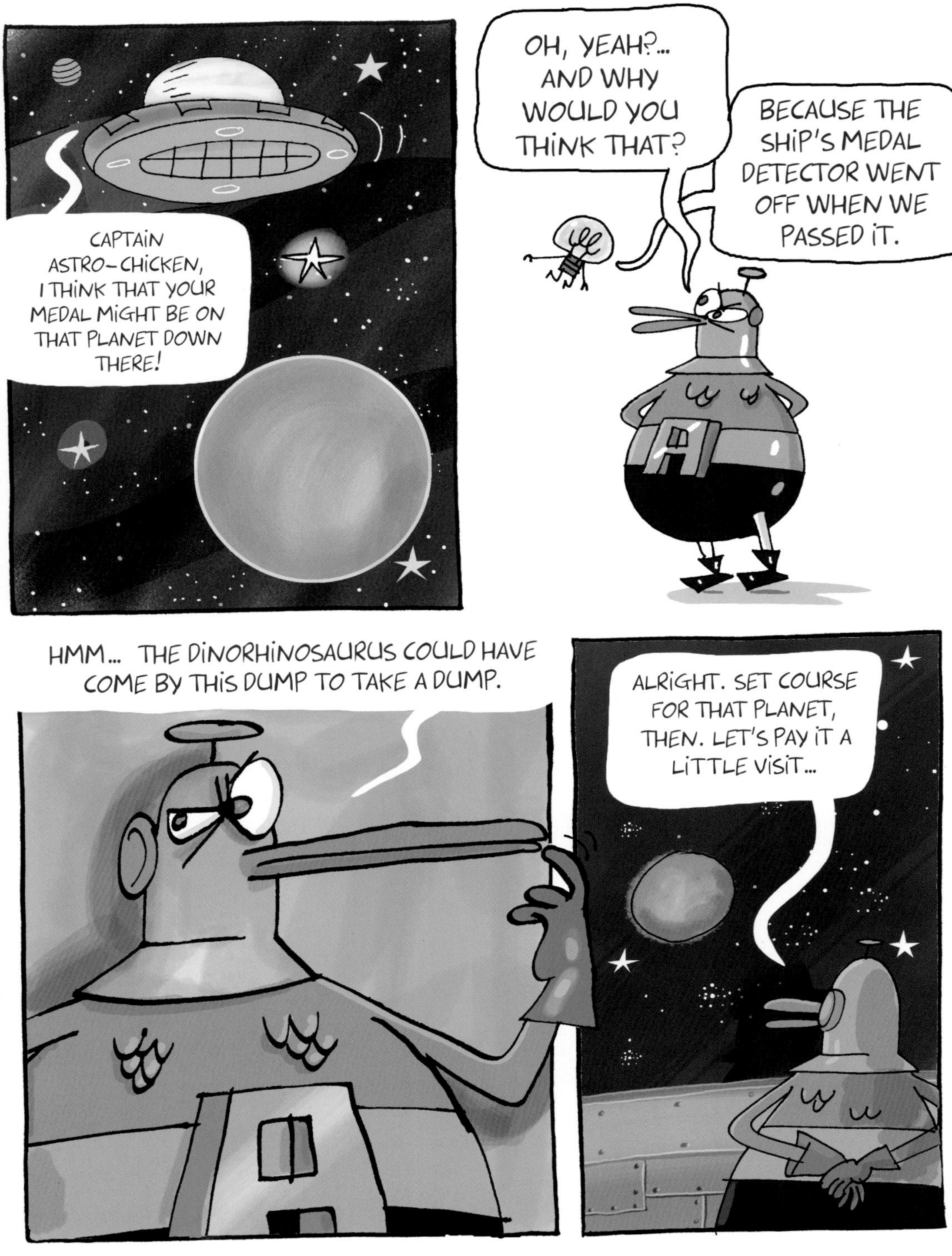
CAPTAIN ASTRO-CHICKEN, I THINK THAT YOUR MEDAL MIGHT BE ON THAT PLANET DOWN THERE!
OH, YEAH?... AND WHY WOULD YOU THINK THAT?
BECAUSE THE SHIP'S MEDAL DETECTOR WENT OFF WHEN WE PASSED IT.
HMM... THE DINORHINOSAURUS COULD HAVE COME BY THIS DUMP TO TAKE A DUMP.
ALRIGHT. SET COURSE FOR THAT PLANET, THEN. LET'S PAY IT A LITTLE VISIT...

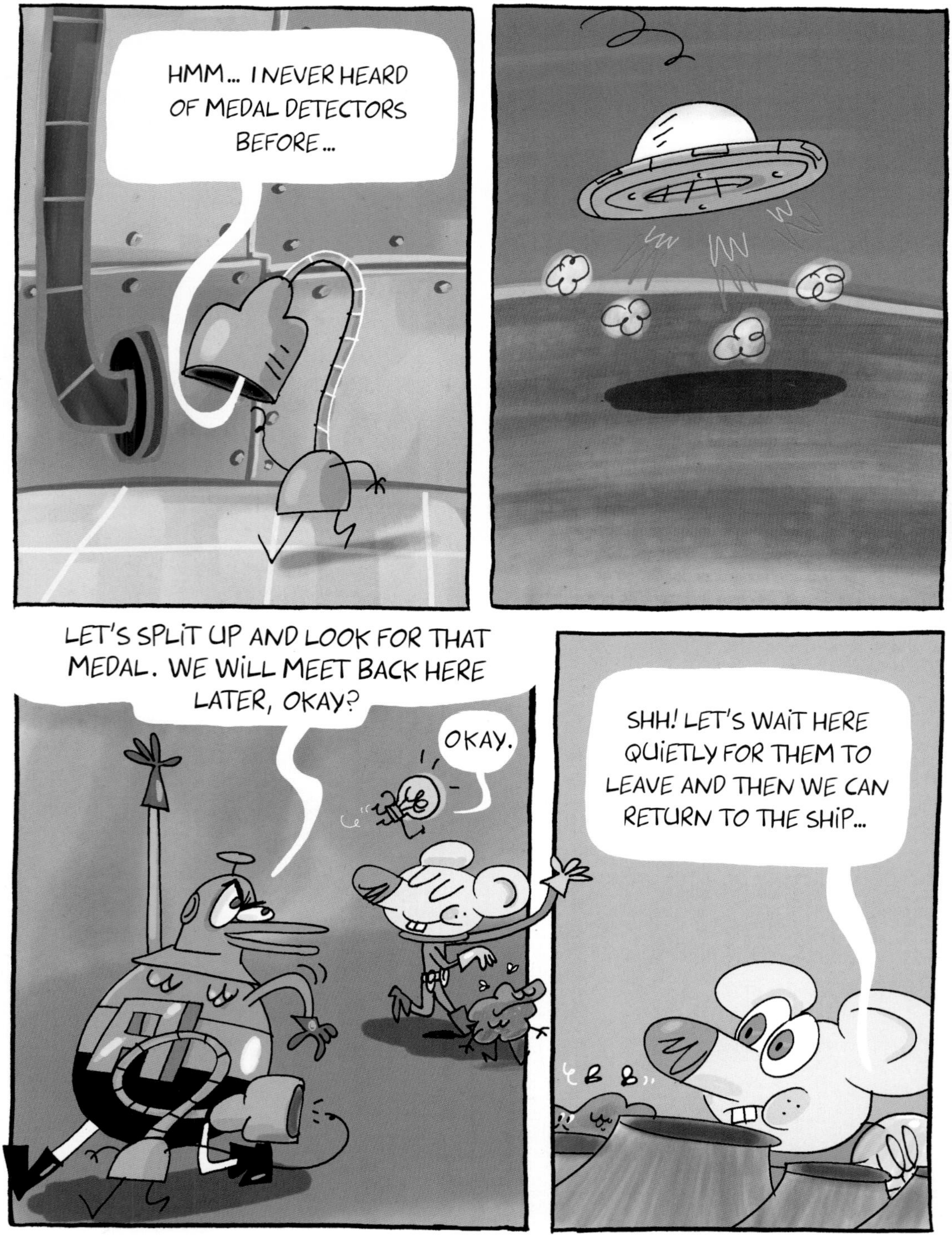

HMM... I NEVER HEARD OF MEDAL DETECTORS BEFORE...
LET'S SPLIT UP AND LOOK FOR THAT MEDAL. WE WILL MEET BACK HERE LATER, OKAY?
OKAY.
SHH! LET'S WAIT HERE QUIETLY FOR THEM TO LEAVE AND THEN WE CAN RETURN TO THE SHIP...

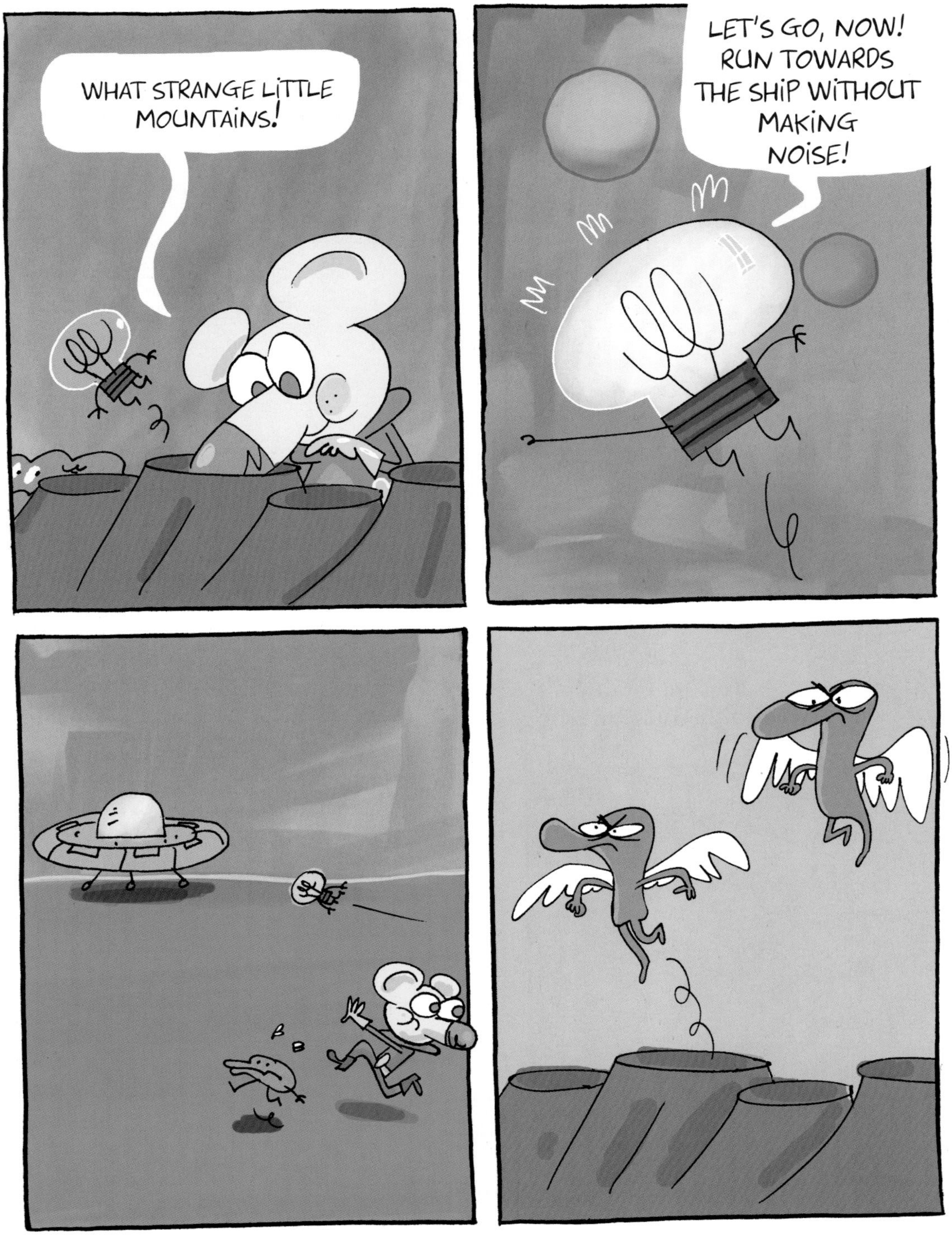
WHAT STRANGE LITTLE MOUNTAINS!
LET'S GO, NOW! RUN TOWARDS THE SHIP WITHOUT MAKING NOISE!

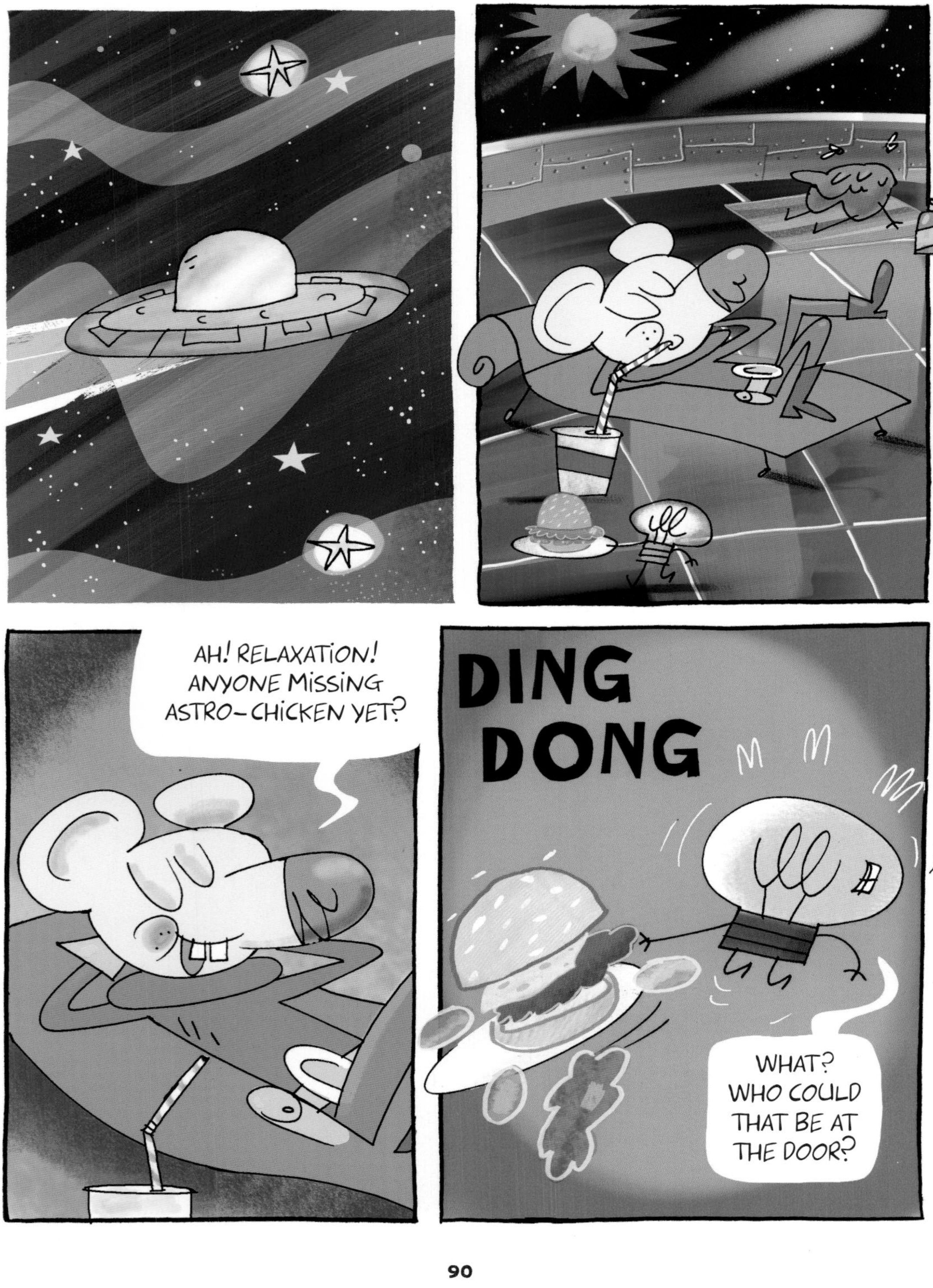
AH! RELAXATION! ANYONE MISSING ASTRO-CHICKEN YET?
DING DONG
WHAT? WHO COULD THAT BE AT THE DOOR?

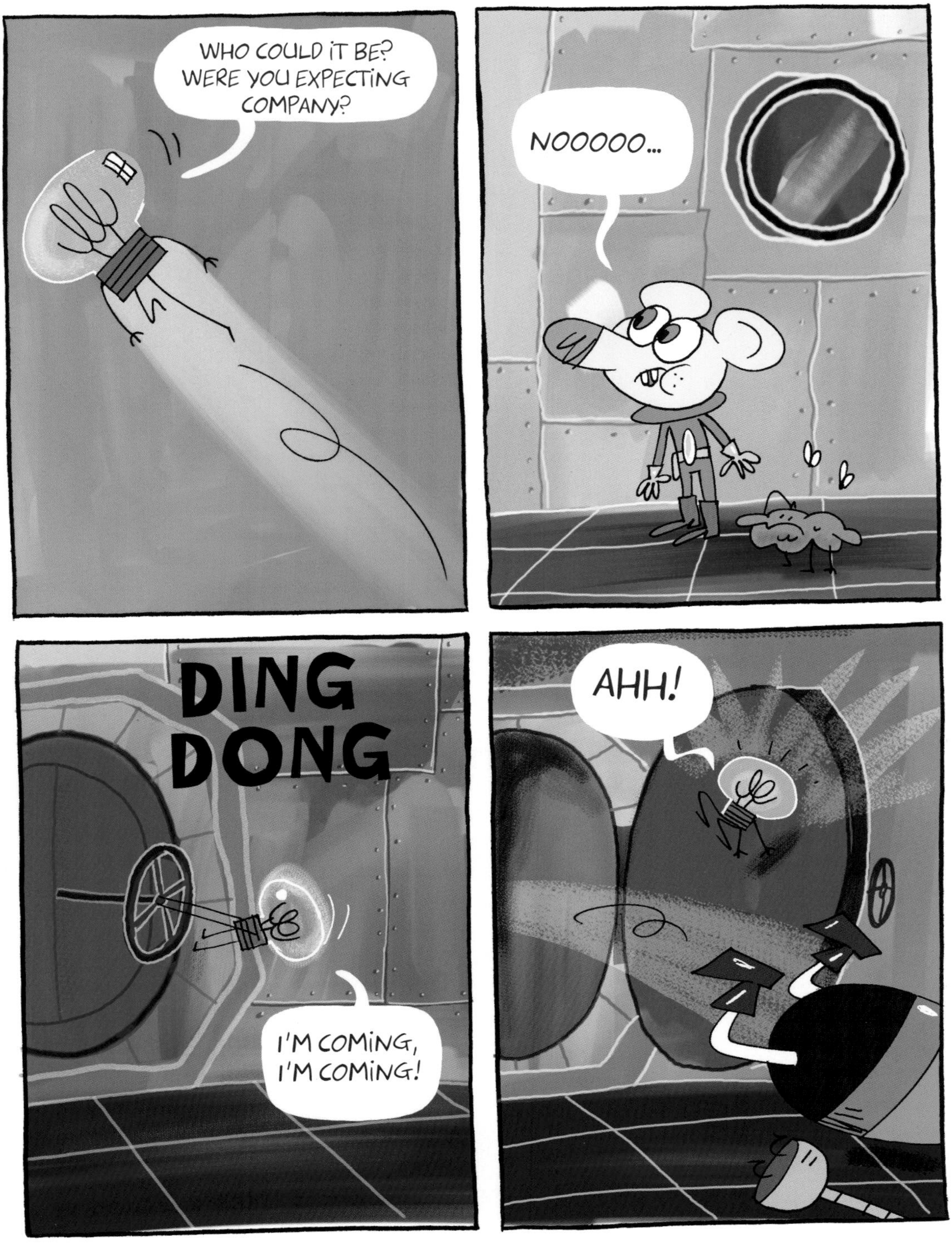
WHO COULD IT BE? WERE YOU EXPECTING COMPANY?
NOOOOO...
DING DONG
I'M COMING, I'M COMING!
AHH!

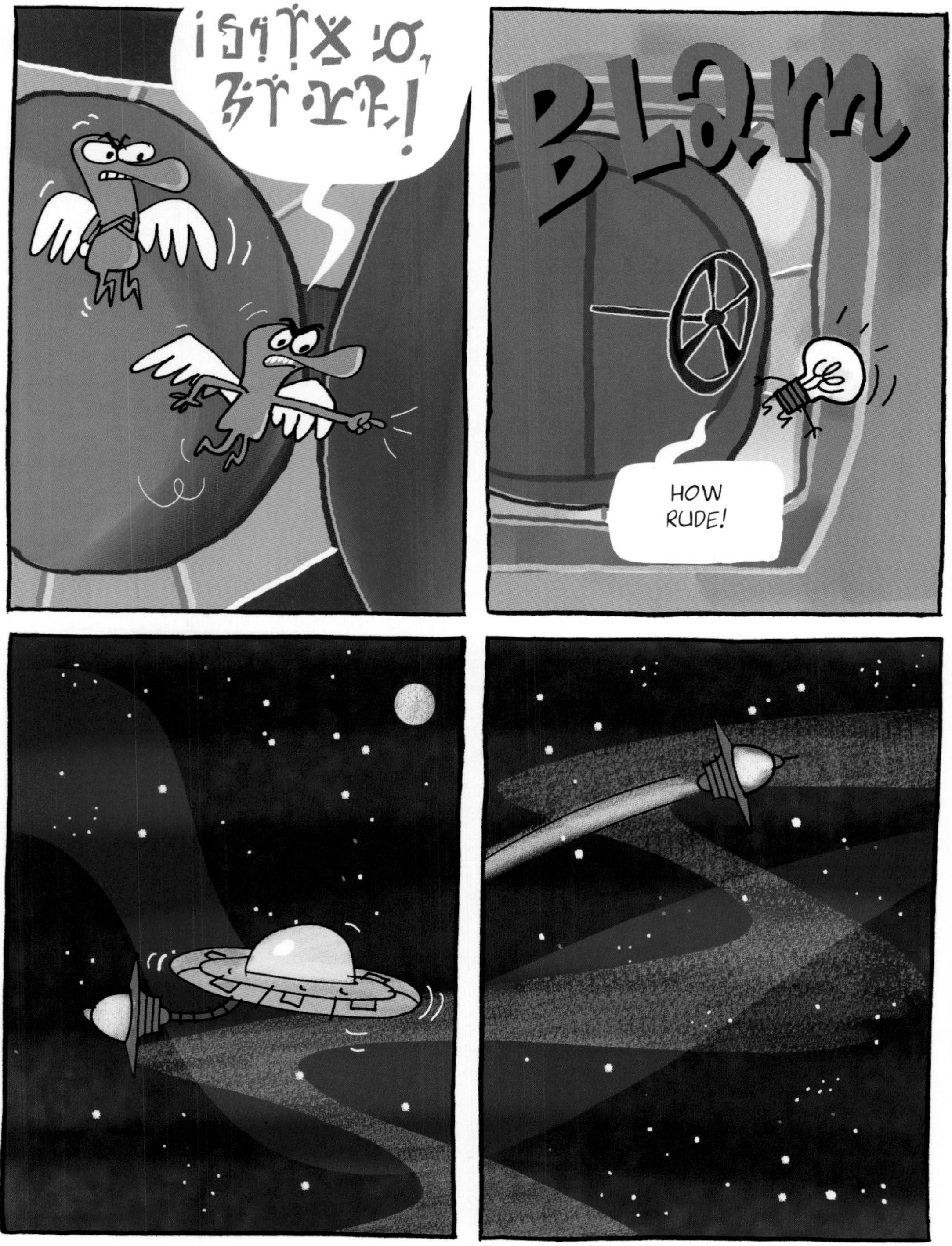
BLAM
HOW RUDE!

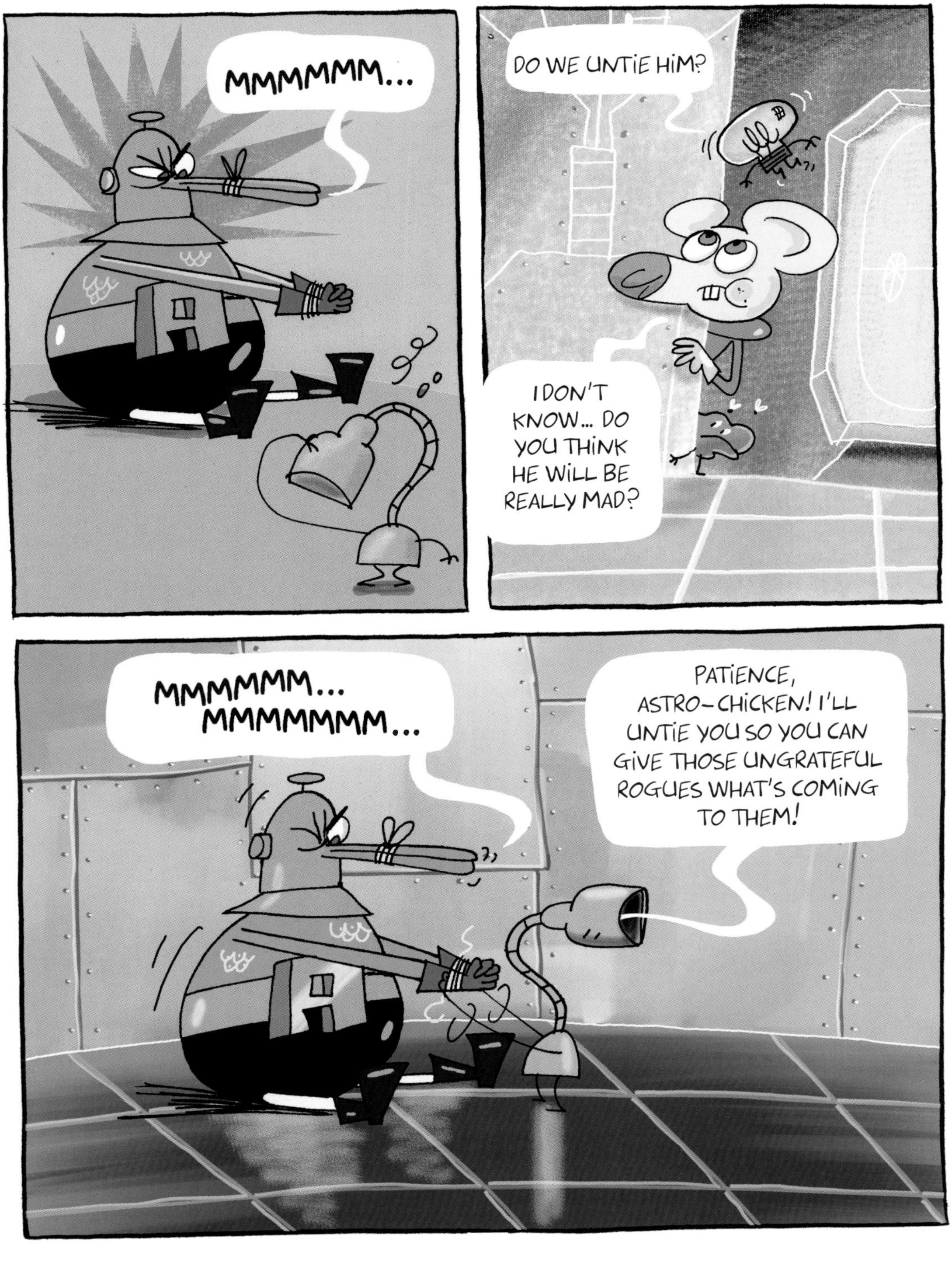
MMMMMM...
DO WE UNTIE HIM?
I DON'T KNOW... DO YOU THINK HE WILL BE REALLY MAD?
MMMMMM... MMMMMMM...
PATIENCE, ASTRO-CHICKEN! I'LL UNTIE YOU SO YOU CAN GIVE THOSE UNGRATEFUL ROGUES WHAT'S COMING TO THEM!

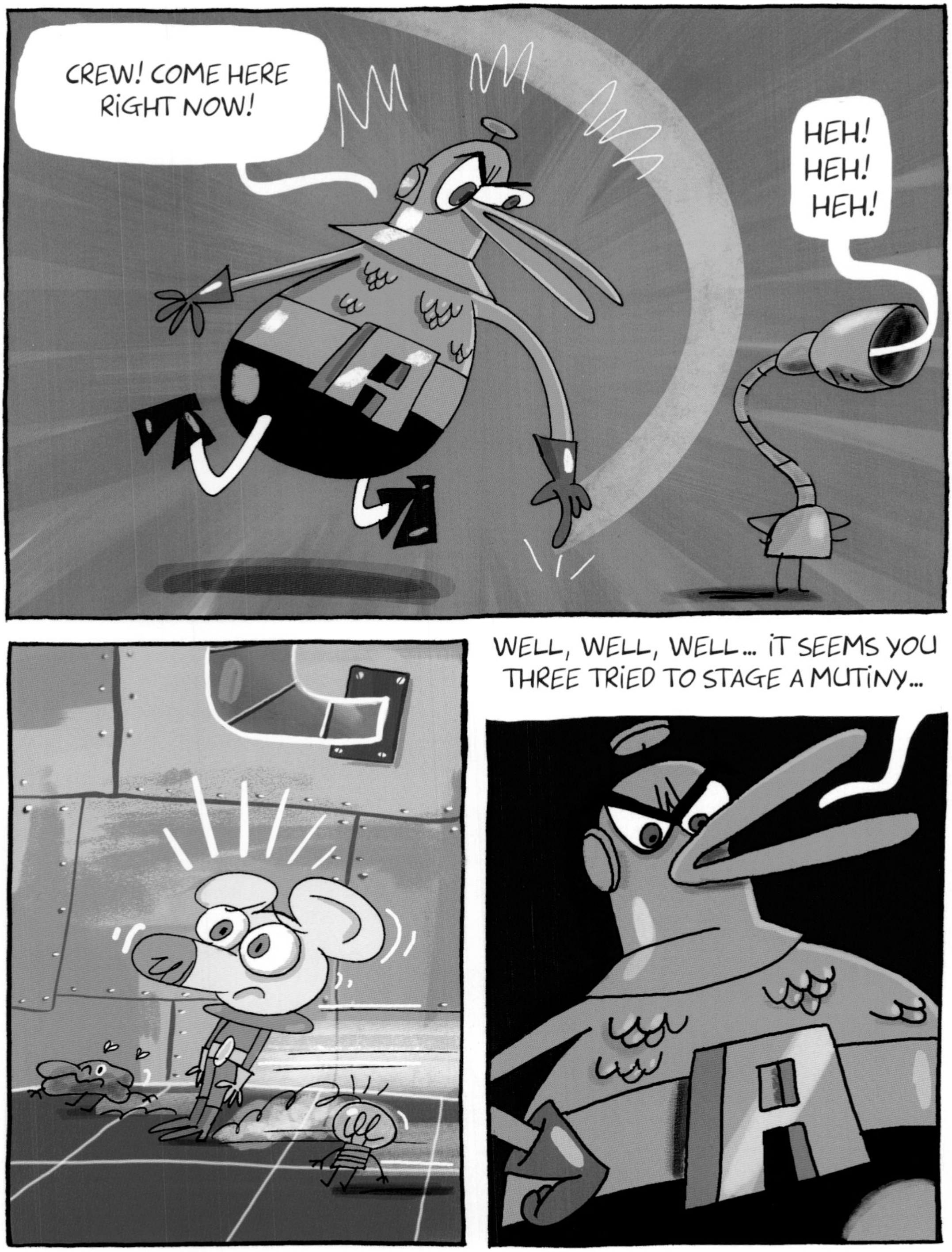
CREW! COME HERE RIGHT NOW!
HEH! HEH! HEH!
WELL, WELL, WELL... IT SEEMS YOU THREE TRIED TO STAGE A MUTINY...

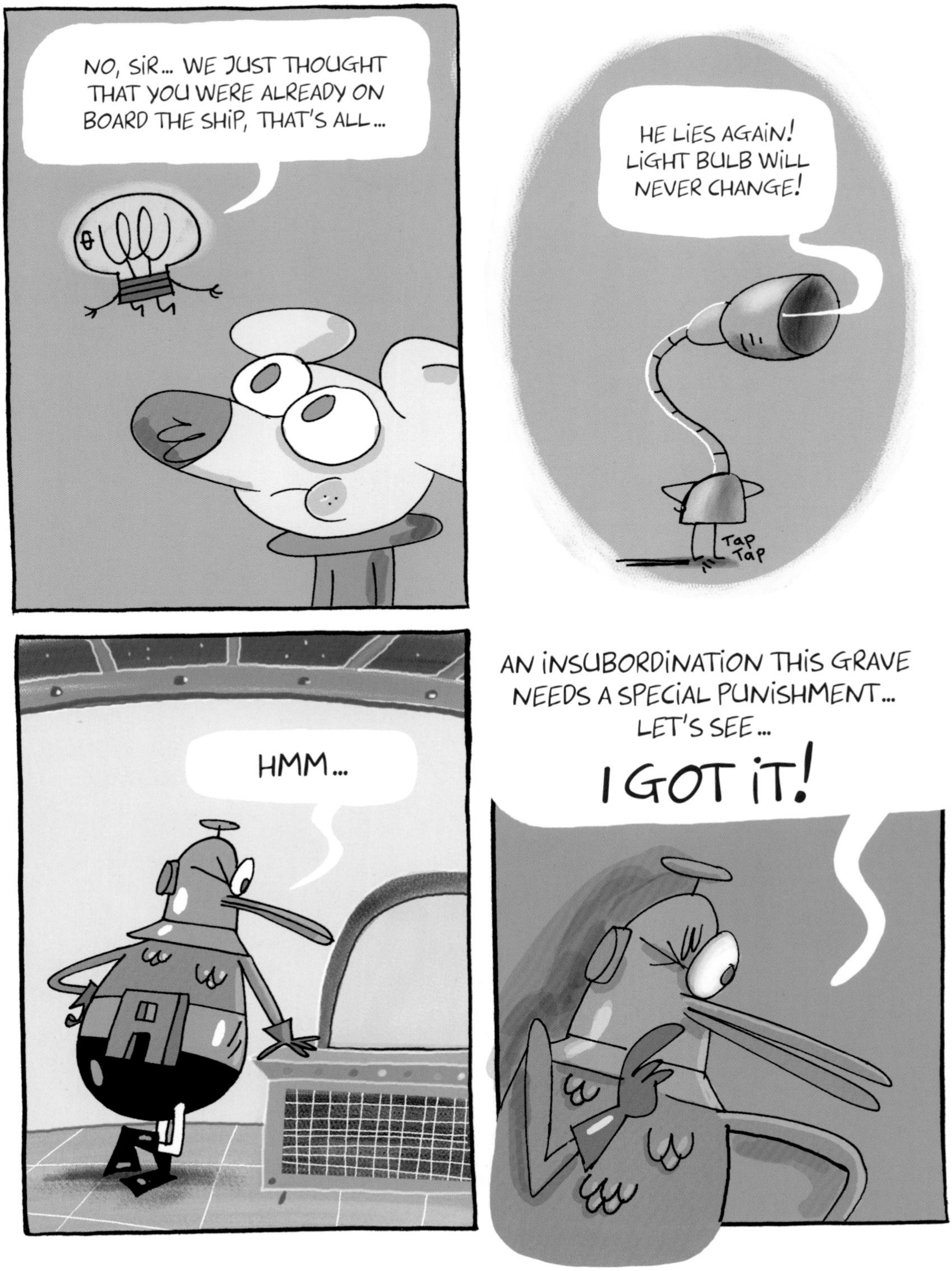
NO, SIR... WE JUST THOUGHT THAT YOU WERE ALREADY ON BOARD THE SHIP, THAT'S ALL...
HE LIES AGAIN! LIGHT BULB WILL NEVER CHANGE!
TAP TAP
HMM...
AN INSUBORDINATION THIS GRAVE NEEDS A SPECIAL PUNISHMENT... LET'S SEE...
I GOT IT!

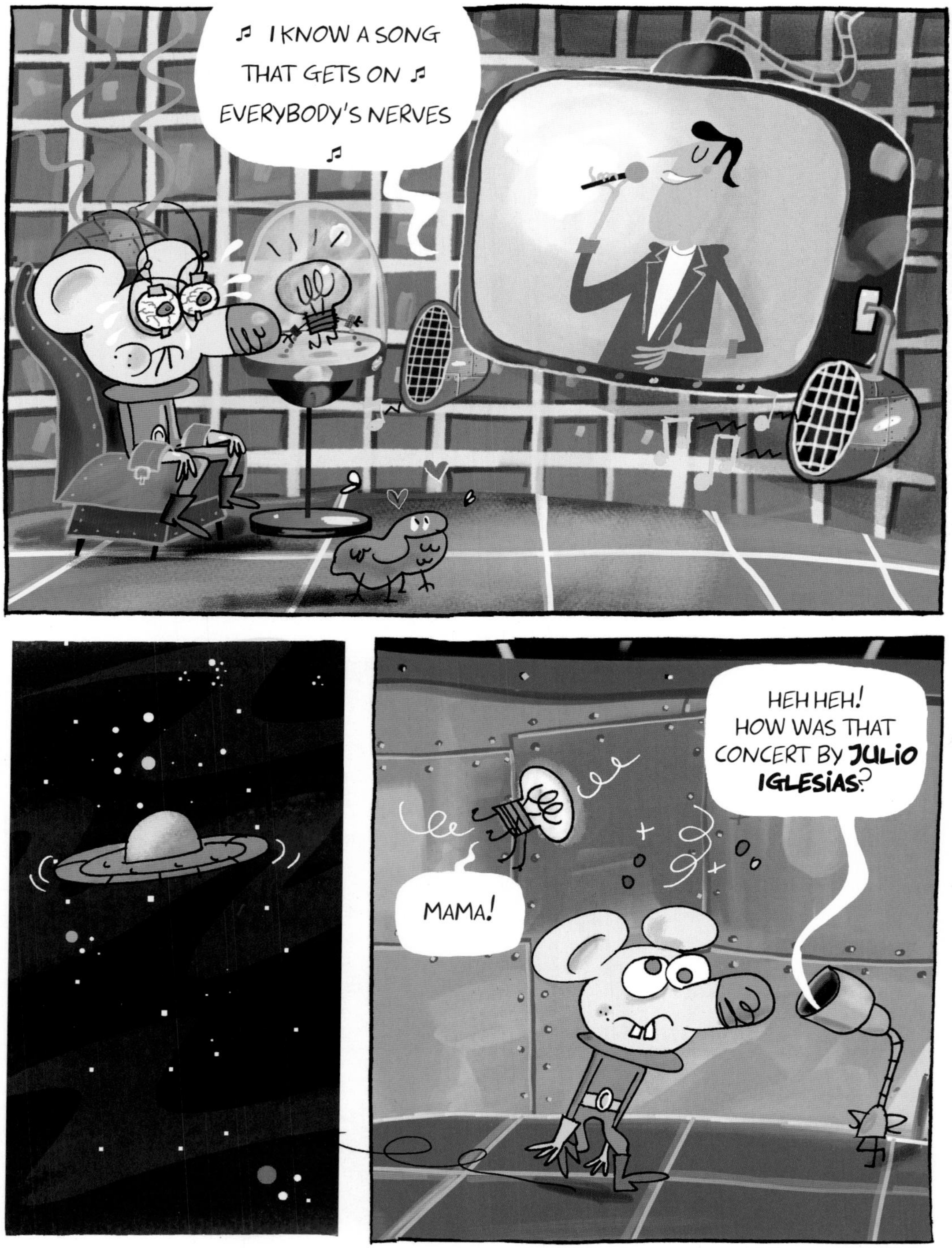
♫ I KNOW A SONG THAT GETS ON ♫ EVERYBODY'S NERVES ♫
HEH HEH! HOW WAS THAT CONCERT BY **JULIO IGLESIAS**?
MAMA!

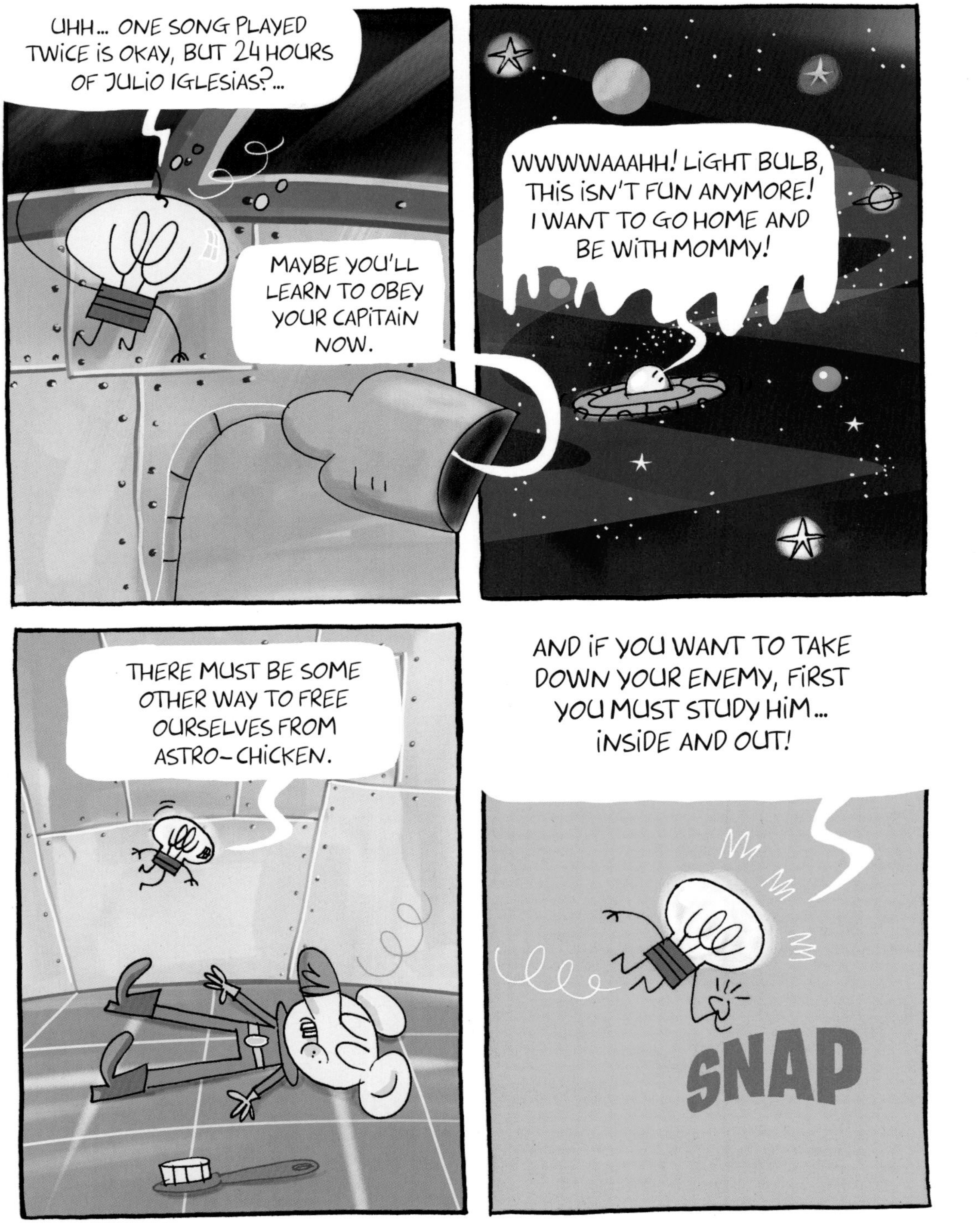
UHH... ONE SONG PLAYED TWICE IS OKAY, BUT 24 HOURS OF JULIO IGLESIAS?...
MAYBE YOU'LL LEARN TO OBEY YOUR CAPITAIN NOW.
WWWWAAAHH! LIGHT BULB, THIS ISN'T FUN ANYMORE! I WANT TO GO HOME AND BE WITH MOMMY!
THERE MUST BE SOME OTHER WAY TO FREE OURSELVES FROM ASTRO-CHICKEN.
AND IF YOU WANT TO TAKE DOWN YOUR ENEMY, FIRST YOU MUST STUDY HIM... INSIDE AND OUT!
SNAP

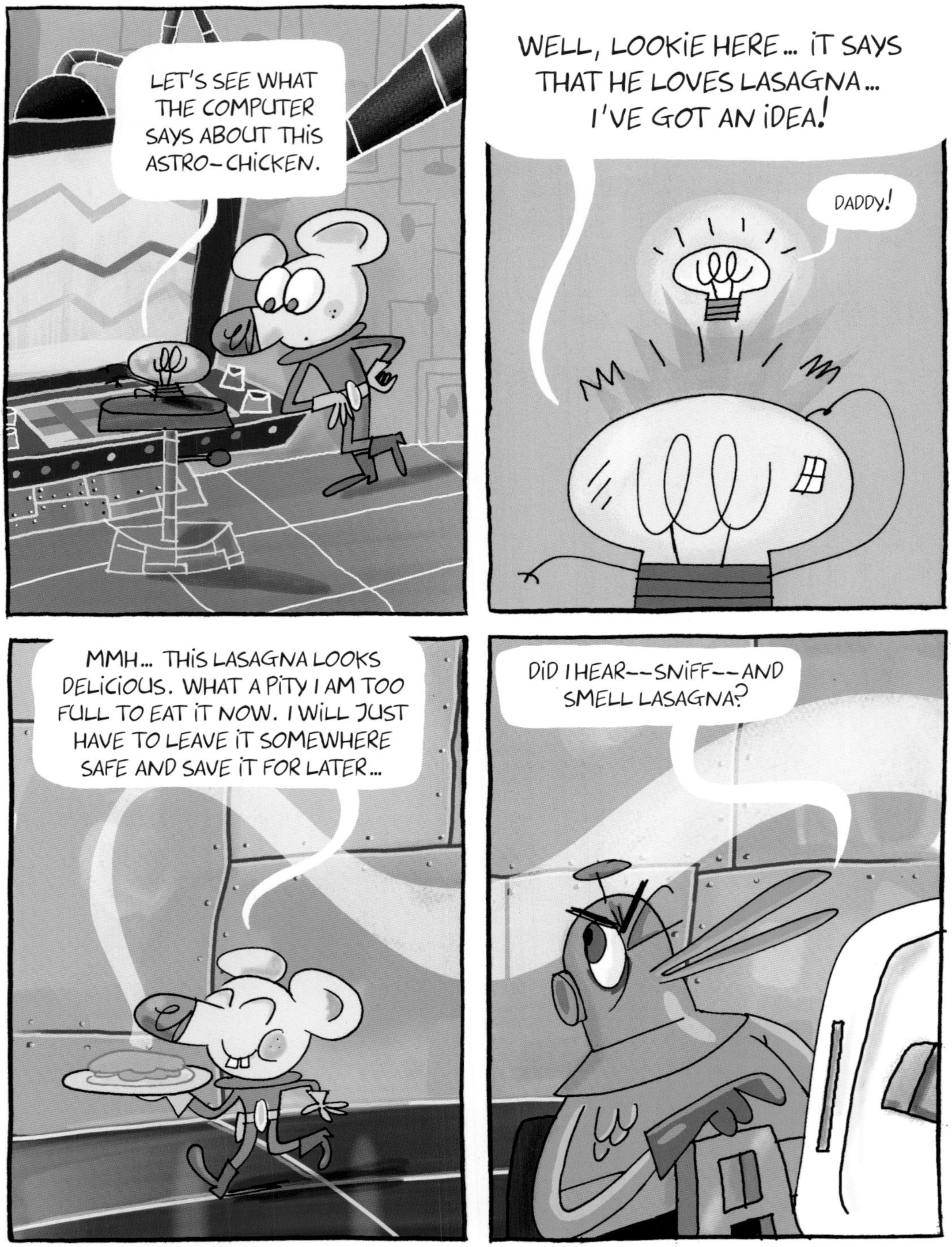
LET'S SEE WHAT THE COMPUTER SAYS ABOUT THIS ASTRO-CHICKEN.
WELL, LOOKIE HERE... IT SAYS THAT HE LOVES LASAGNA... I'VE GOT AN IDEA!
DADDY!
MMH... THIS LASAGNA LOOKS DELICIOUS. WHAT A PITY I AM TOO FULL TO EAT IT NOW. I WILL JUST HAVE TO LEAVE IT SOMEWHERE SAFE AND SAVE IT FOR LATER...
DID I HEAR--SNIFF--AND SMELL LASAGNA?

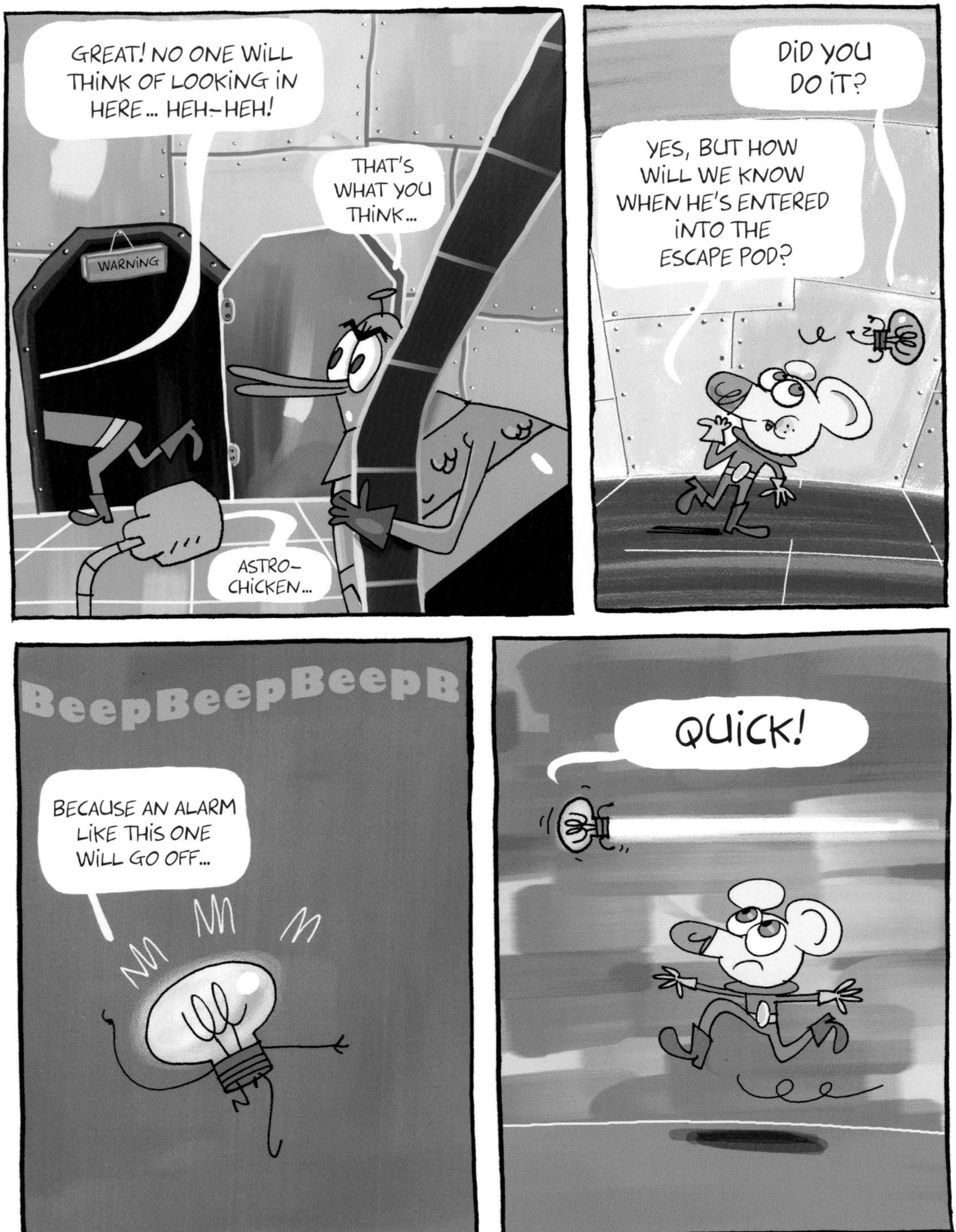
GREAT! NO ONE WILL THINK OF LOOKING IN HERE... HEH-HEH!
WARNING
THAT'S WHAT YOU THINK...
ASTRO-CHICKEN...
DID YOU DO IT?
YES, BUT HOW WILL WE KNOW WHEN HE'S ENTERED INTO THE ESCAPE POD?
BeepBeepBeepB
BECAUSE AN ALARM LIKE THIS ONE WILL GO OFF...
QUICK!

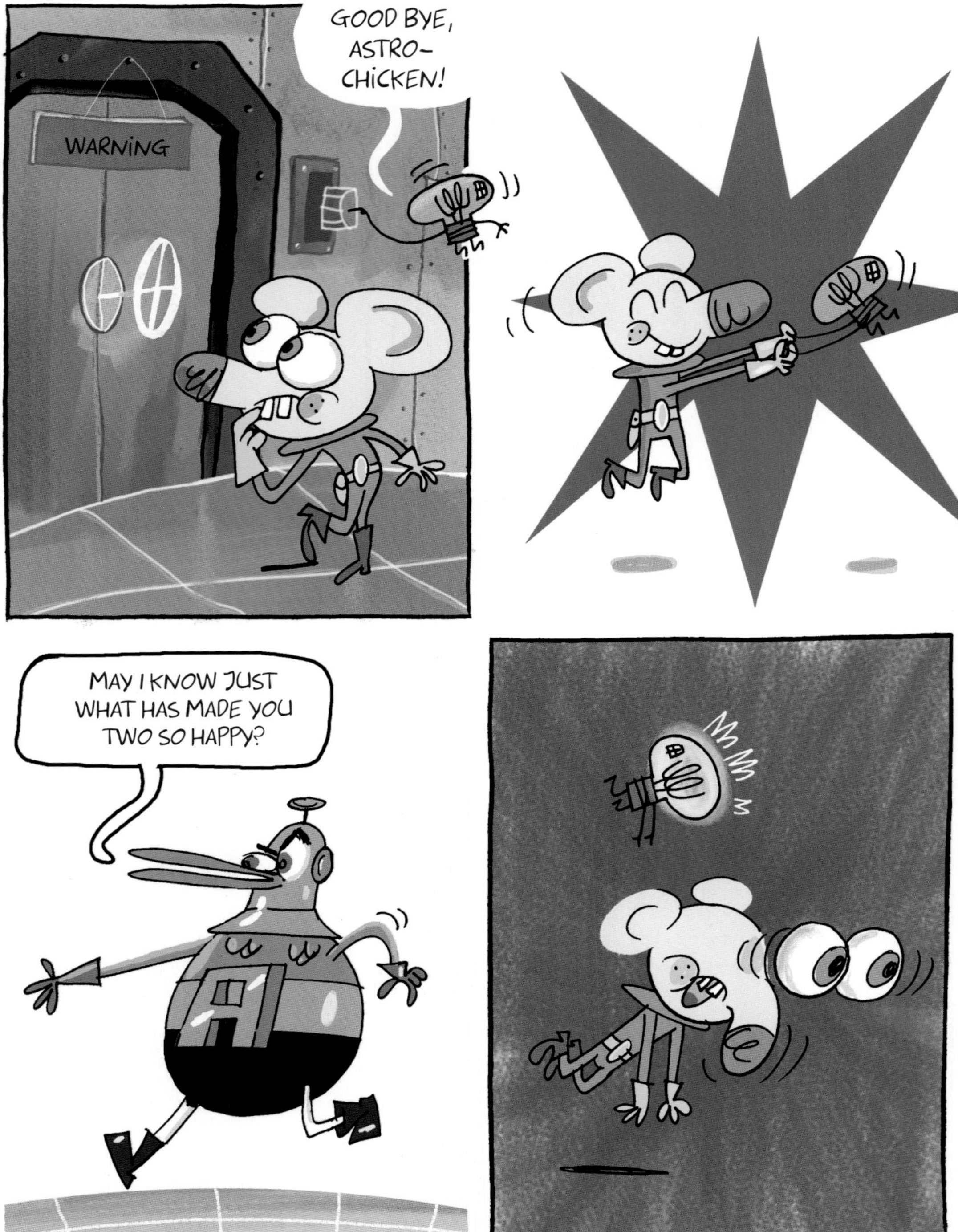
GOOD BYE, ASTRO-CHICKEN!
WARNING
MAY I KNOW JUST WHAT HAS MADE YOU TWO SO HAPPY?

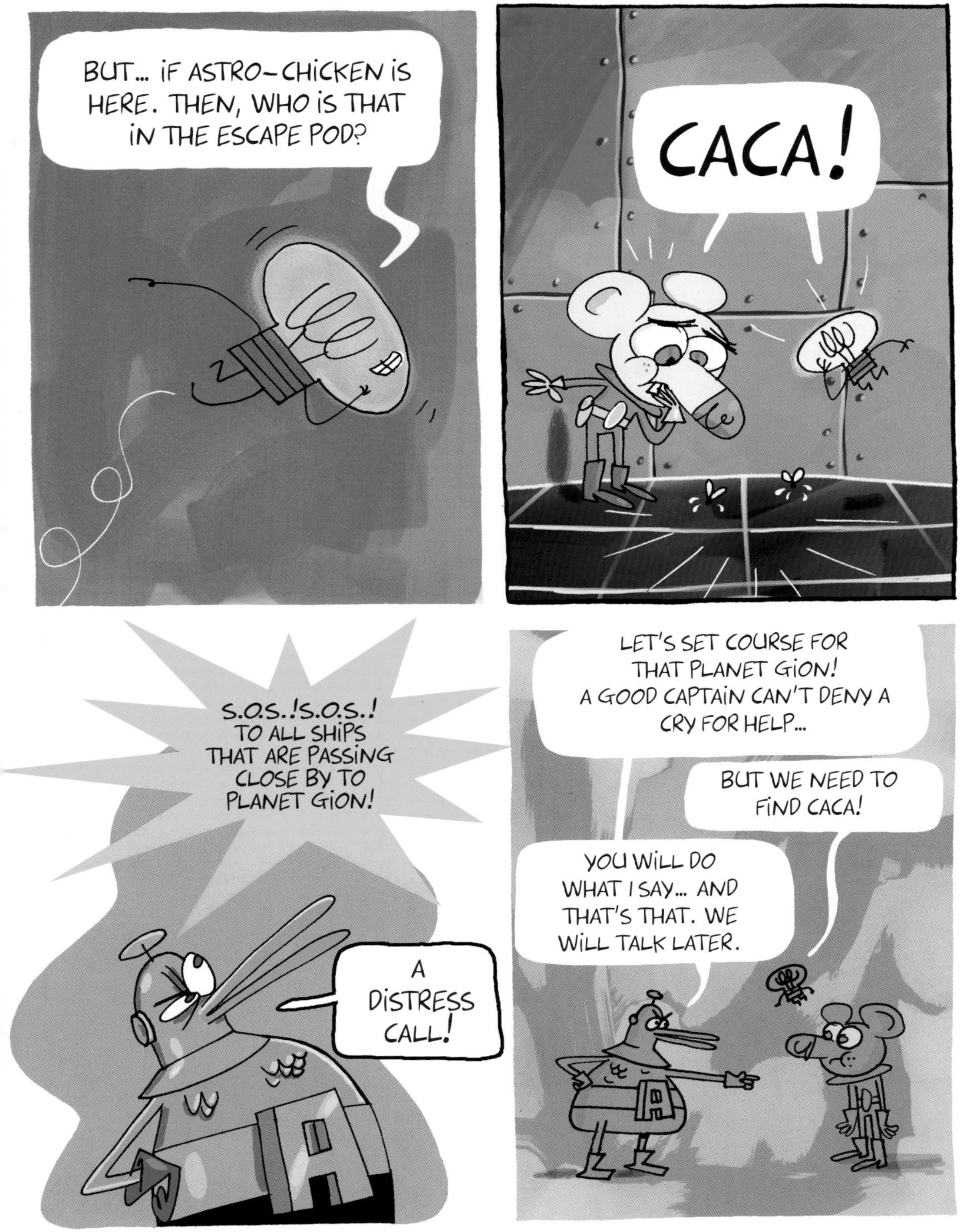
BUT... IF ASTRO-CHICKEN IS HERE. THEN, WHO IS THAT IN THE ESCAPE POD?
CACA!
S.O.S..!S.O.S..! TO ALL SHIPS THAT ARE PASSING CLOSE BY TO PLANET GION!
A DISTRESS CALL!
LET'S SET COURSE FOR THAT PLANET GION! A GOOD CAPTAIN CAN'T DENY A CRY FOR HELP...
BUT WE NEED TO FIND CACA!
YOU WILL DO WHAT I SAY... AND THAT'S THAT. WE WILL TALK LATER.

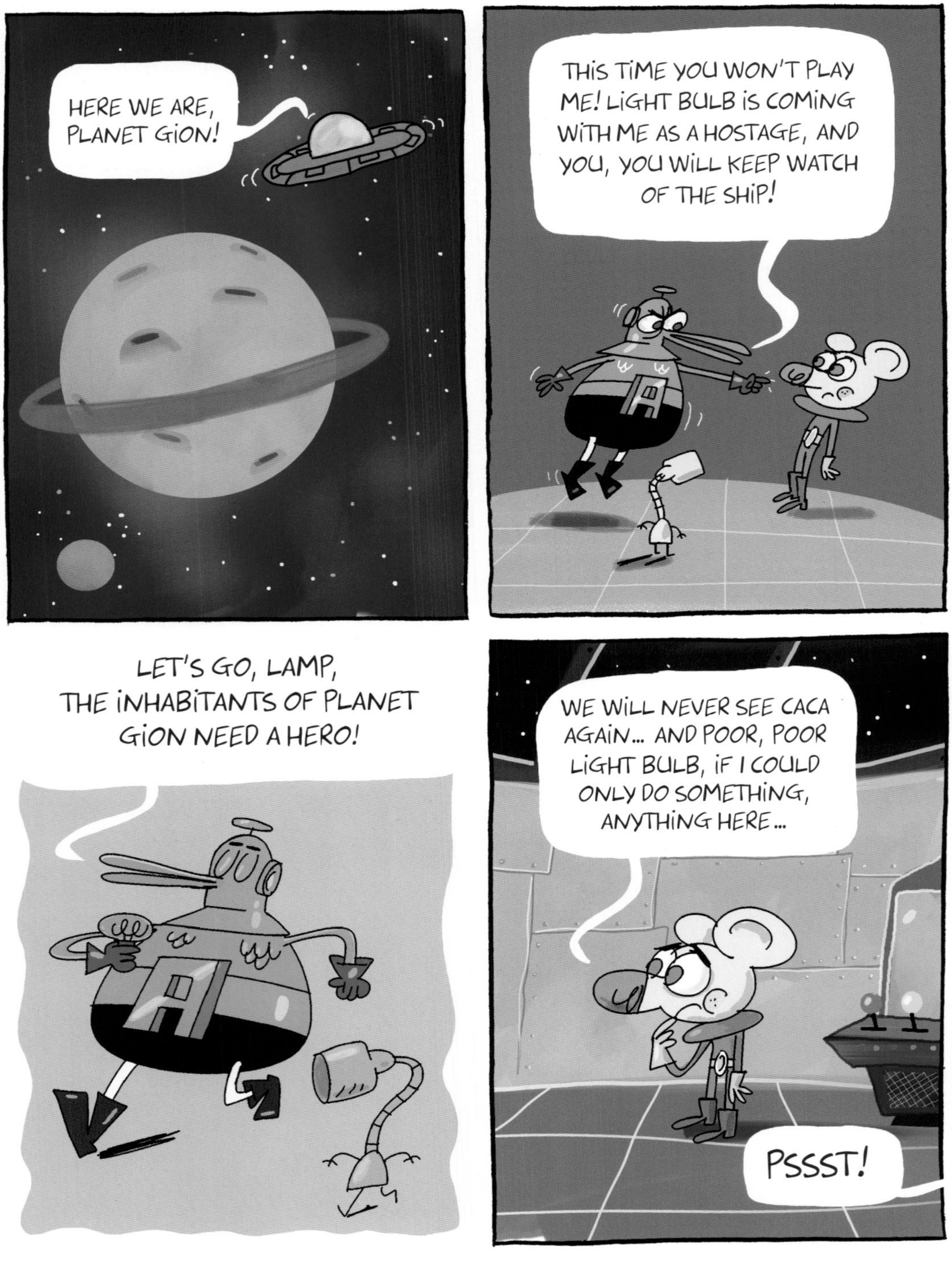
HERE WE ARE, PLANET GION!
THIS TIME YOU WON'T PLAY ME! LIGHT BULB IS COMING WITH ME AS A HOSTAGE, AND YOU, YOU WILL KEEP WATCH OF THE SHIP!
LET'S GO, LAMP, THE INHABITANTS OF PLANET GION NEED A HERO!
WE WILL NEVER SEE CACA AGAIN... AND POOR, POOR LIGHT BULB, IF I COULD ONLY DO SOMETHING, ANYTHING HERE...
PSSST!

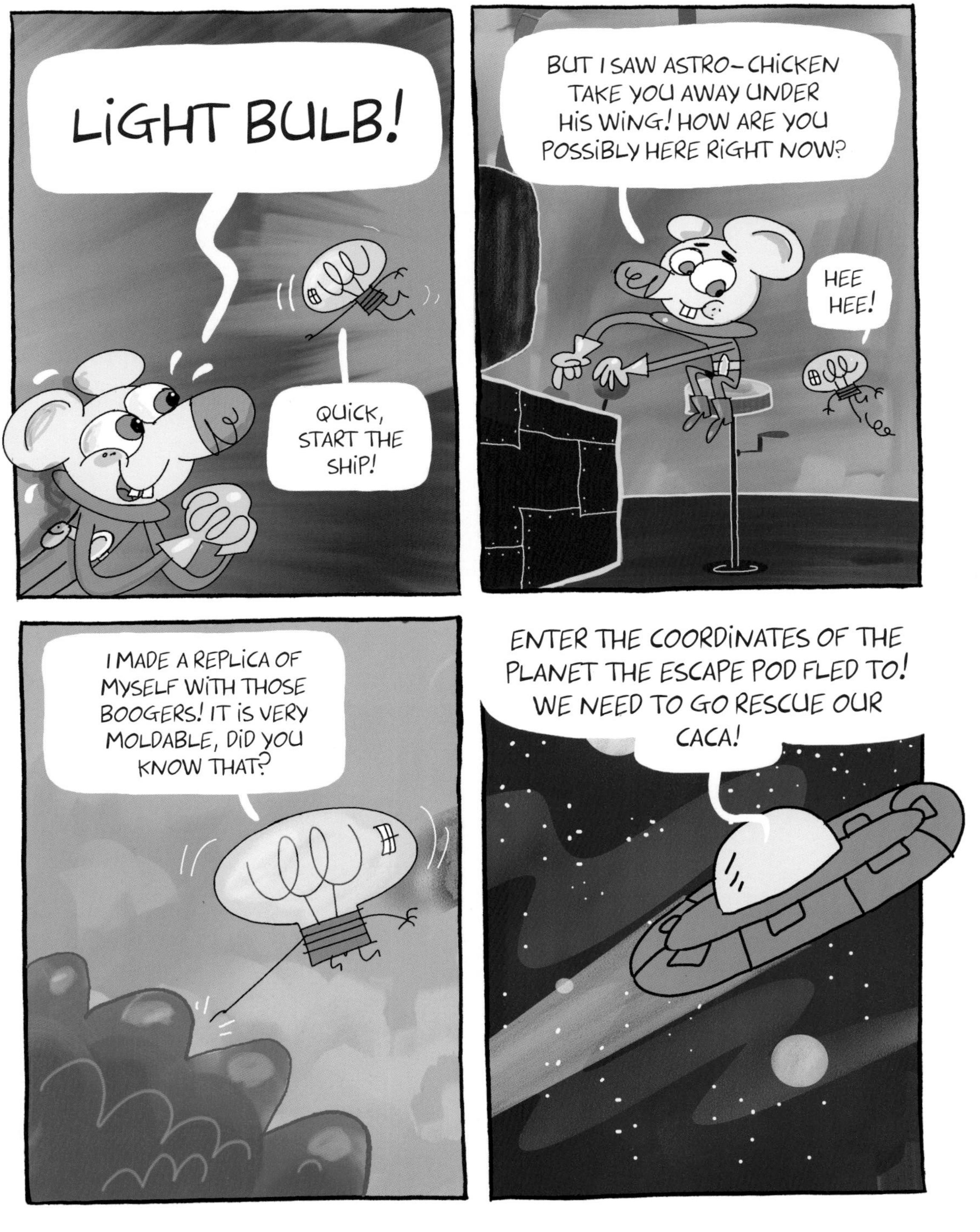
LIGHT BULB!
QUICK, START THE SHIP!
BUT I SAW ASTRO-CHICKEN TAKE YOU AWAY UNDER HIS WING! HOW ARE YOU POSSIBLY HERE RIGHT NOW?
HEE HEE!
I MADE A REPLICA OF MYSELF WITH THOSE BOOGERS! IT IS VERY MOLDABLE, DID YOU KNOW THAT?
ENTER THE COORDINATES OF THE PLANET THE ESCAPE POD FLED TO! WE NEED TO GO RESCUE OUR CACA!

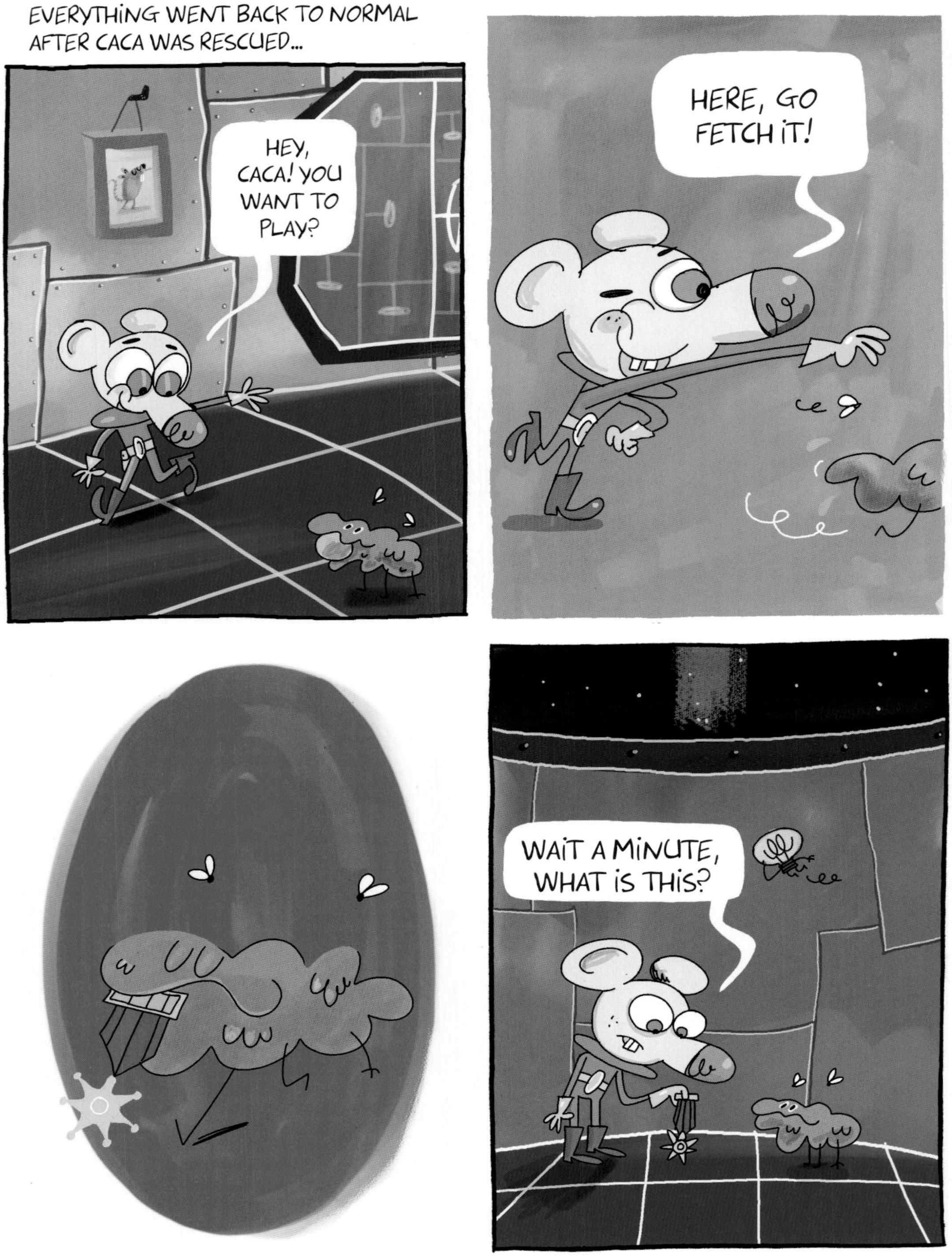
EVERYTHING WENT BACK TO NORMAL AFTER CACA WAS RESCUED...
HEY, CACA! YOU WANT TO PLAY?
HERE, GO FETCH IT!
WAIT A MINUTE, WHAT IS THIS?

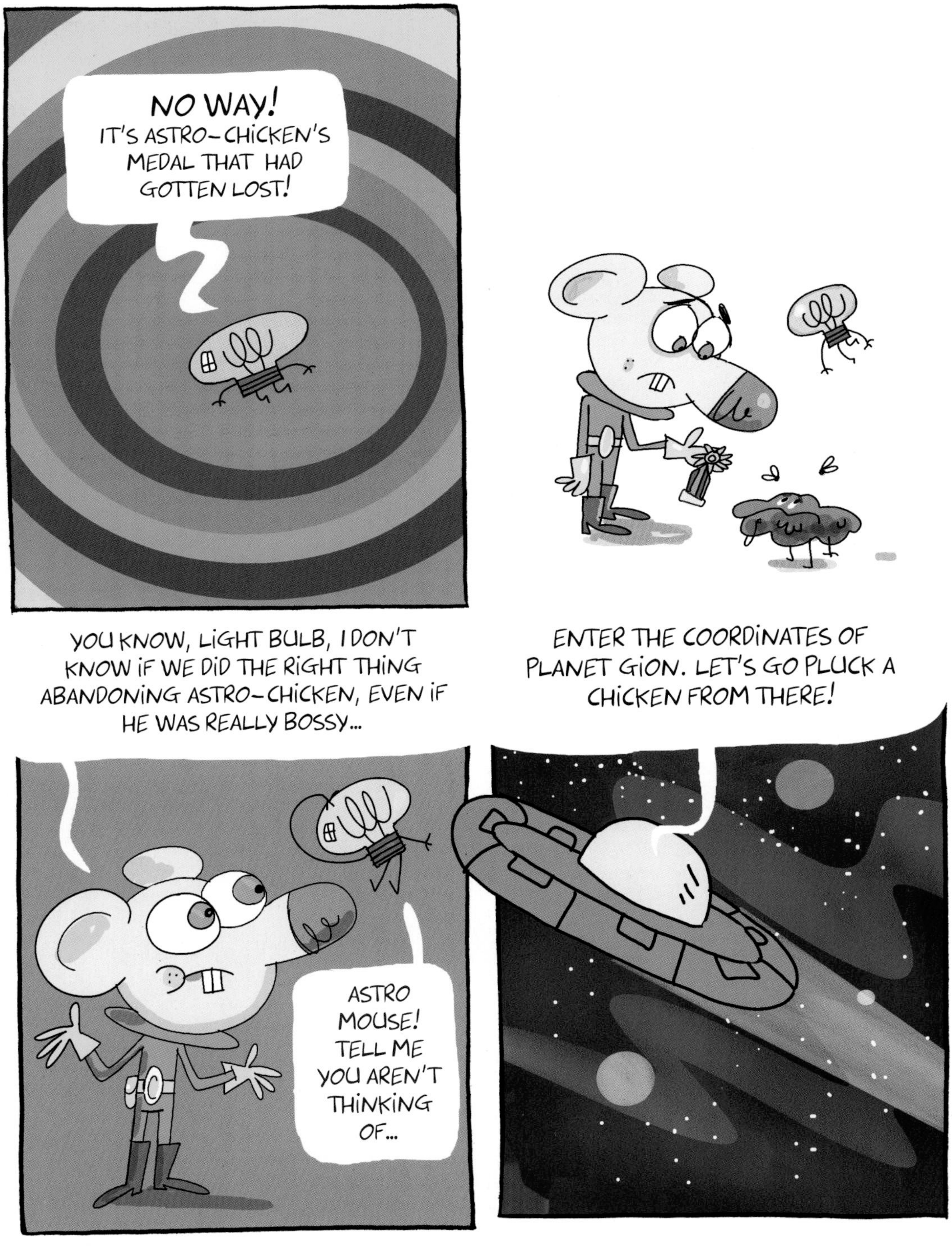
NO WAY! IT'S ASTRO-CHICKEN'S MEDAL THAT HAD GOTTEN LOST!
YOU KNOW, LIGHT BULB, I DON'T KNOW IF WE DID THE RIGHT THING ABANDONING ASTRO-CHICKEN, EVEN IF HE WAS REALLY BOSSY...
ASTRO MOUSE! TELL ME YOU AREN'T THINKING OF...
ENTER THE COORDINATES OF PLANET GION. LET'S GO PLUCK A CHICKEN FROM THERE!

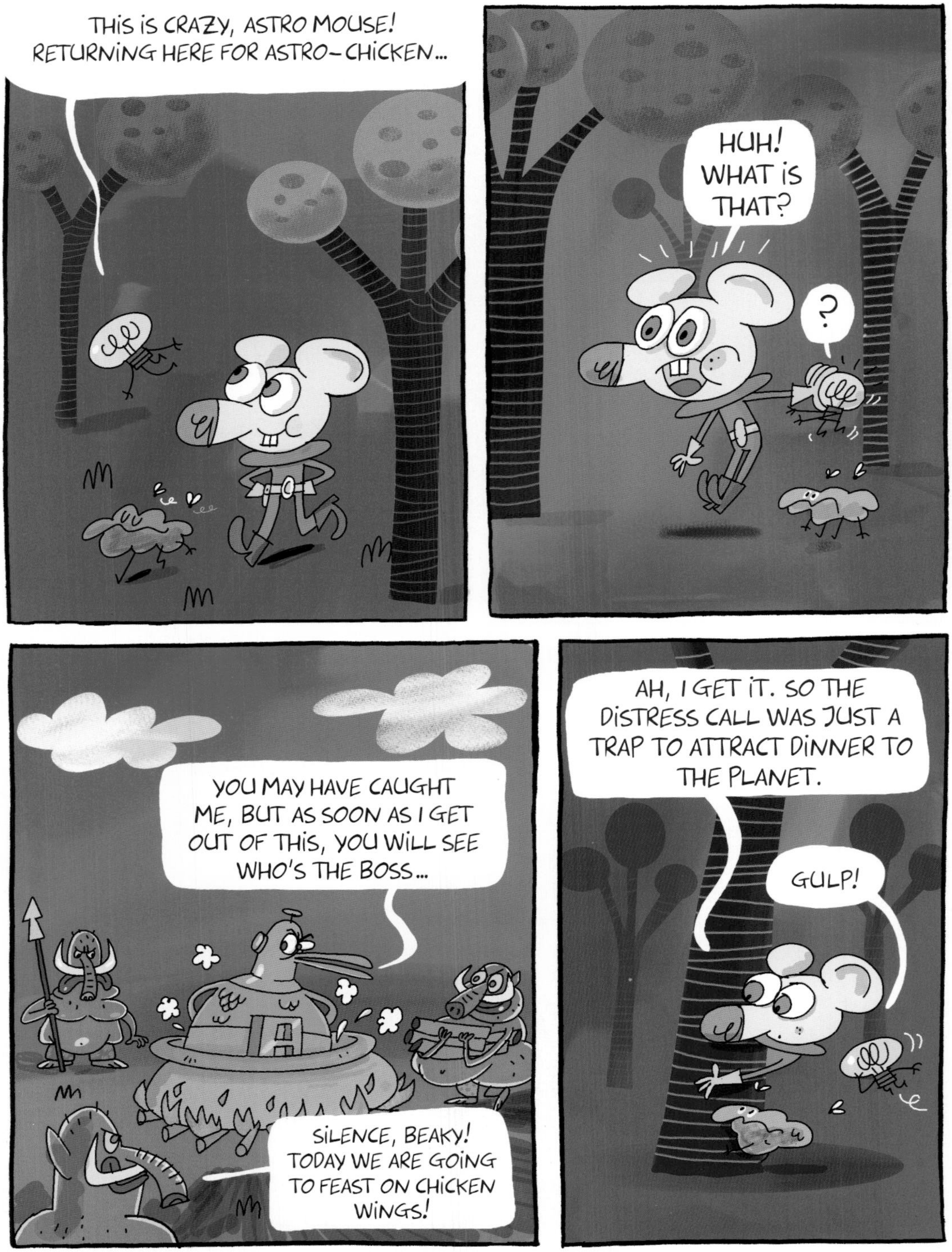
THIS IS CRAZY, ASTRO MOUSE! RETURNING HERE FOR ASTRO-CHICKEN...
HUH! WHAT IS THAT?
?
YOU MAY HAVE CAUGHT ME, BUT AS SOON AS I GET OUT OF THIS, YOU WILL SEE WHO'S THE BOSS...
SILENCE, BEAKY! TODAY WE ARE GOING TO FEAST ON CHICKEN WINGS!
AH, I GET IT. SO THE DISTRESS CALL WAS JUST A TRAP TO ATTRACT DINNER TO THE PLANET.
GULP!

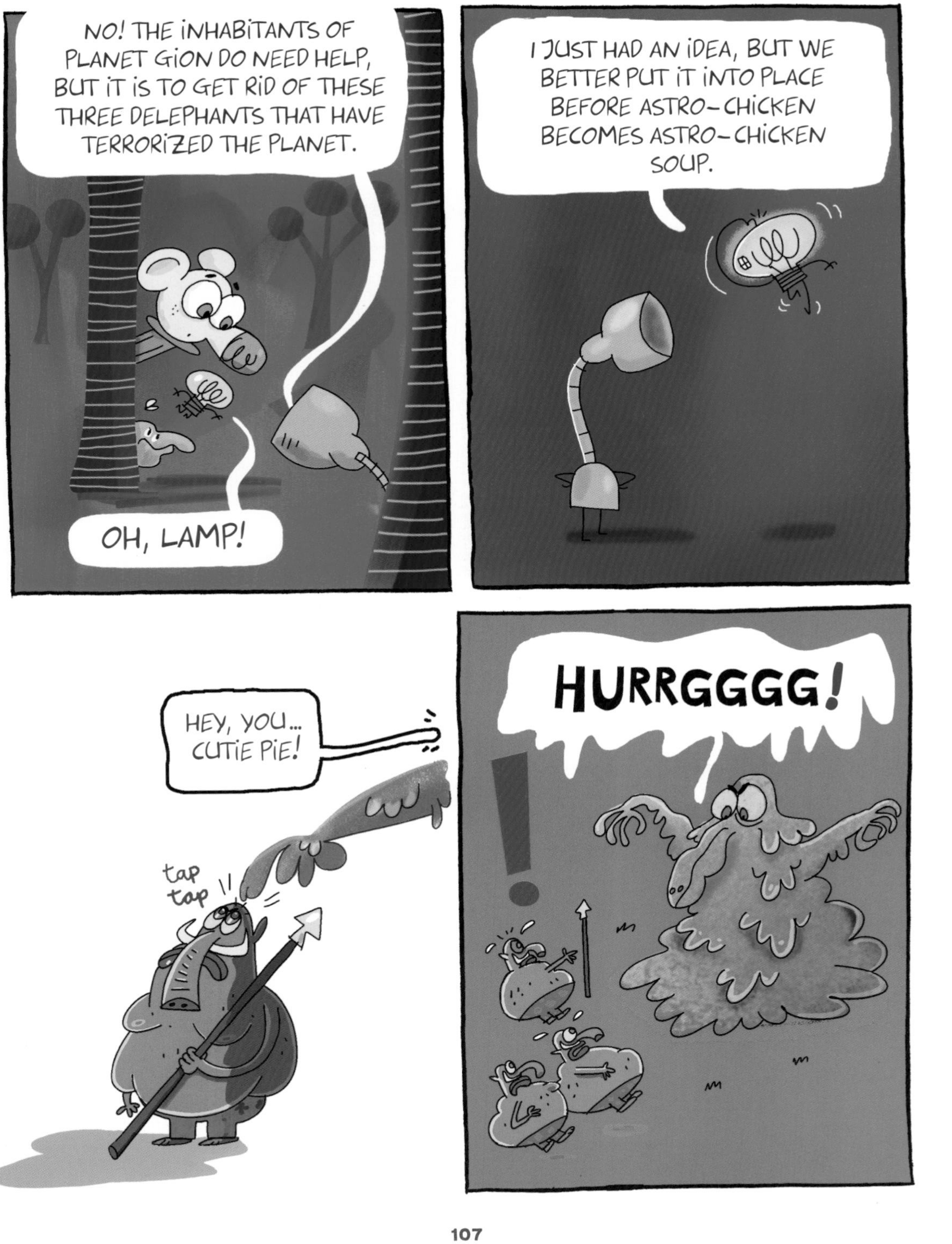
NO! THE INHABITANTS OF PLANET GION DO NEED HELP, BUT IT IS TO GET RID OF THESE THREE DELEPHANTS THAT HAVE TERRORIZED THE PLANET.
OH, LAMP!
I JUST HAD AN IDEA, BUT WE BETTER PUT IT INTO PLACE BEFORE ASTRO-CHICKEN BECOMES ASTRO-CHICKEN SOUP.
HEY, YOU... CUTIE PIE!
tap tap
HURRGGGG!

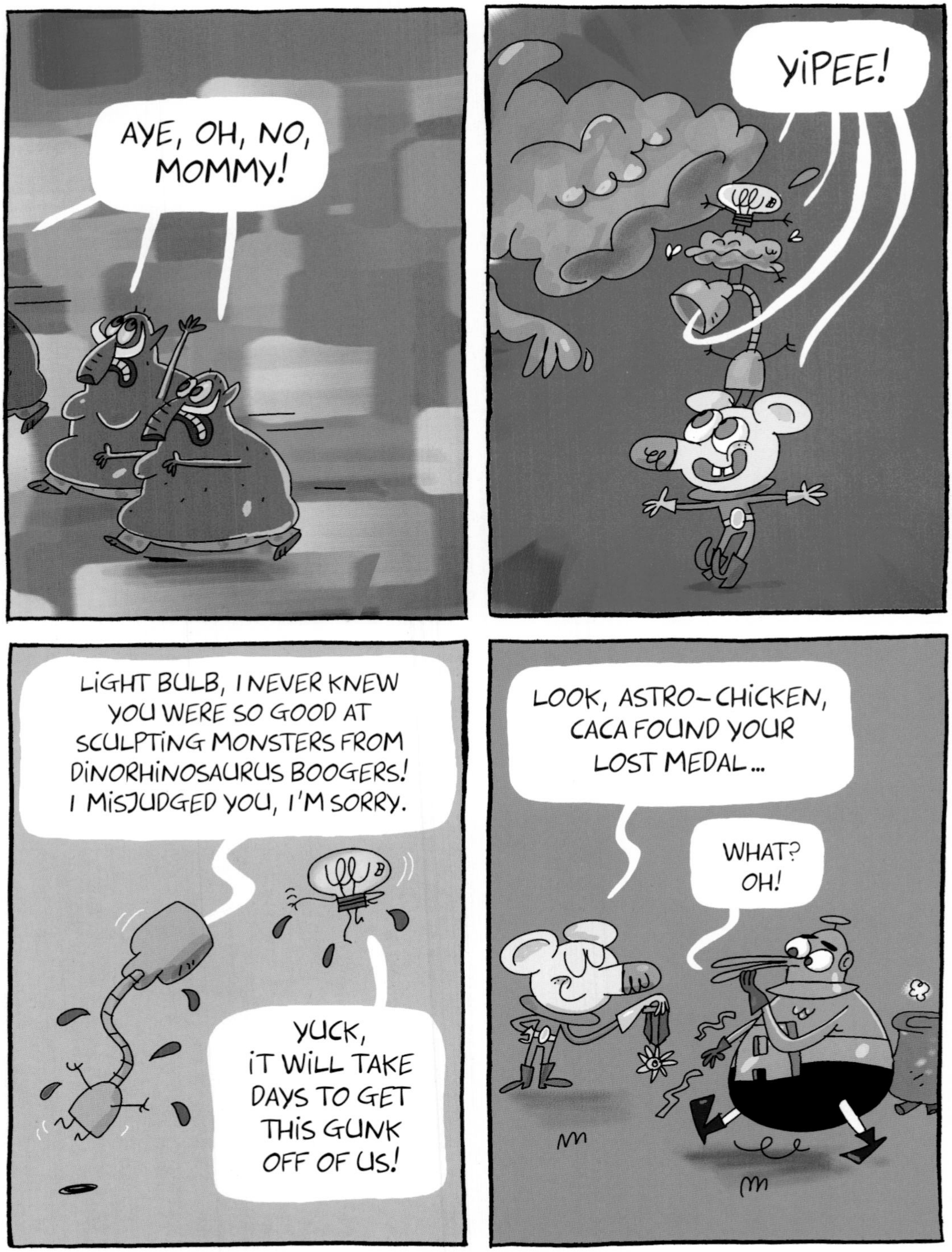
AYE, OH, NO, MOMMY!
YiPEE!
LiGHT BULB, I NEVER KNEW YOU WERE SO GOOD AT SCULPTiNG MONSTERS FROM DiNORHiNOSAURUS BOOGERS! I MiSJUDGED YOU, I'M SORRY.
YUCK, iT WiLL TAKE DAYS TO GET THiS GUNK OFF OF US!
LOOK, ASTRO-CHiCKEN, CACA FOUND YOUR LOST MEDAL...
WHAT? OH!

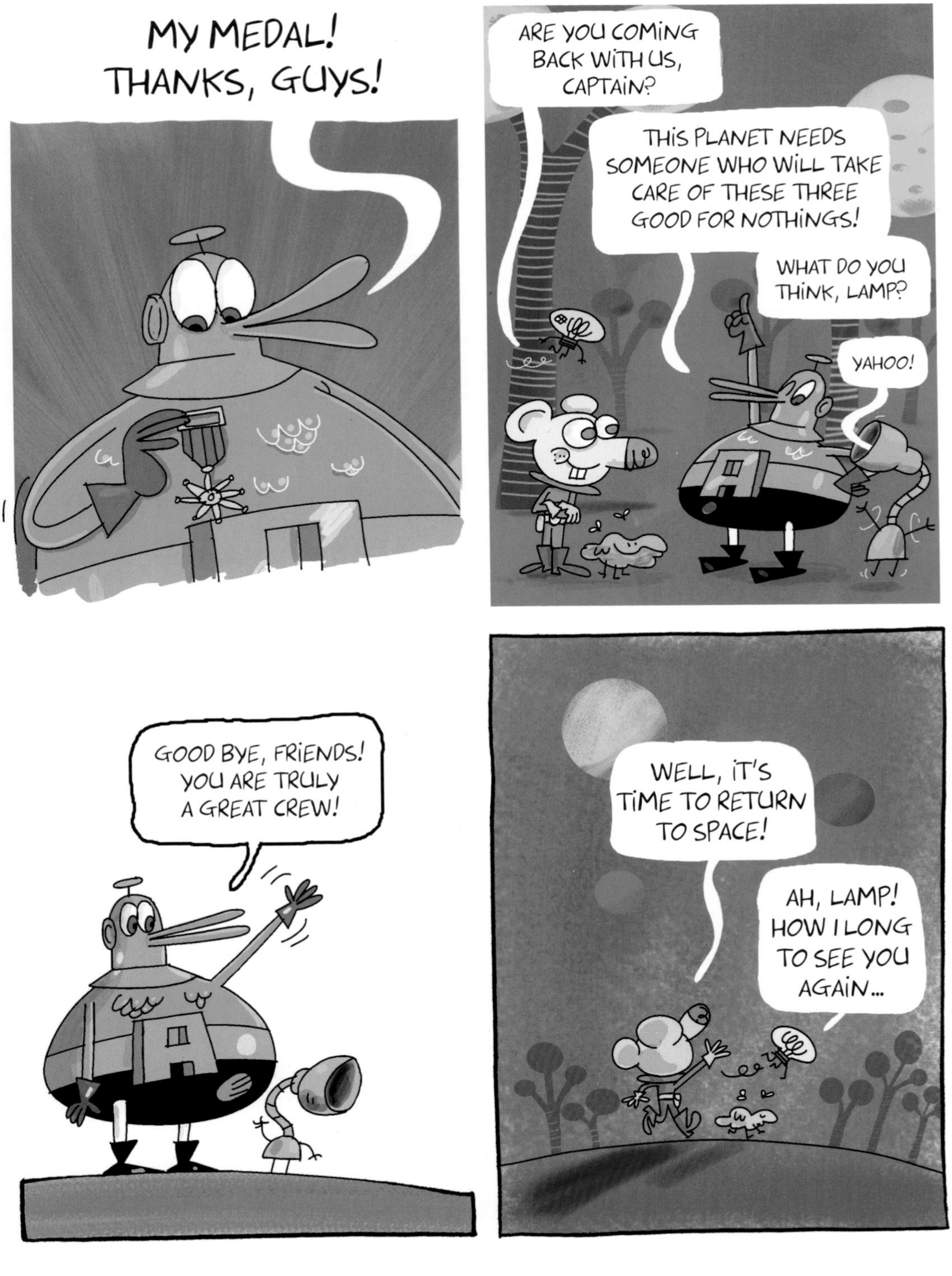
MY MEDAL! THANKS, GUYS!
ARE YOU COMING BACK WITH US, CAPTAIN?
THIS PLANET NEEDS SOMEONE WHO WILL TAKE CARE OF THESE THREE GOOD FOR NOTHINGS!
WHAT DO YOU THINK, LAMP?
YAHOO!
GOOD BYE, FRIENDS! YOU ARE TRULY A GREAT CREW!
WELL, IT'S TIME TO RETURN TO SPACE!
AH, LAMP! HOW I LONG TO SEE YOU AGAIN...

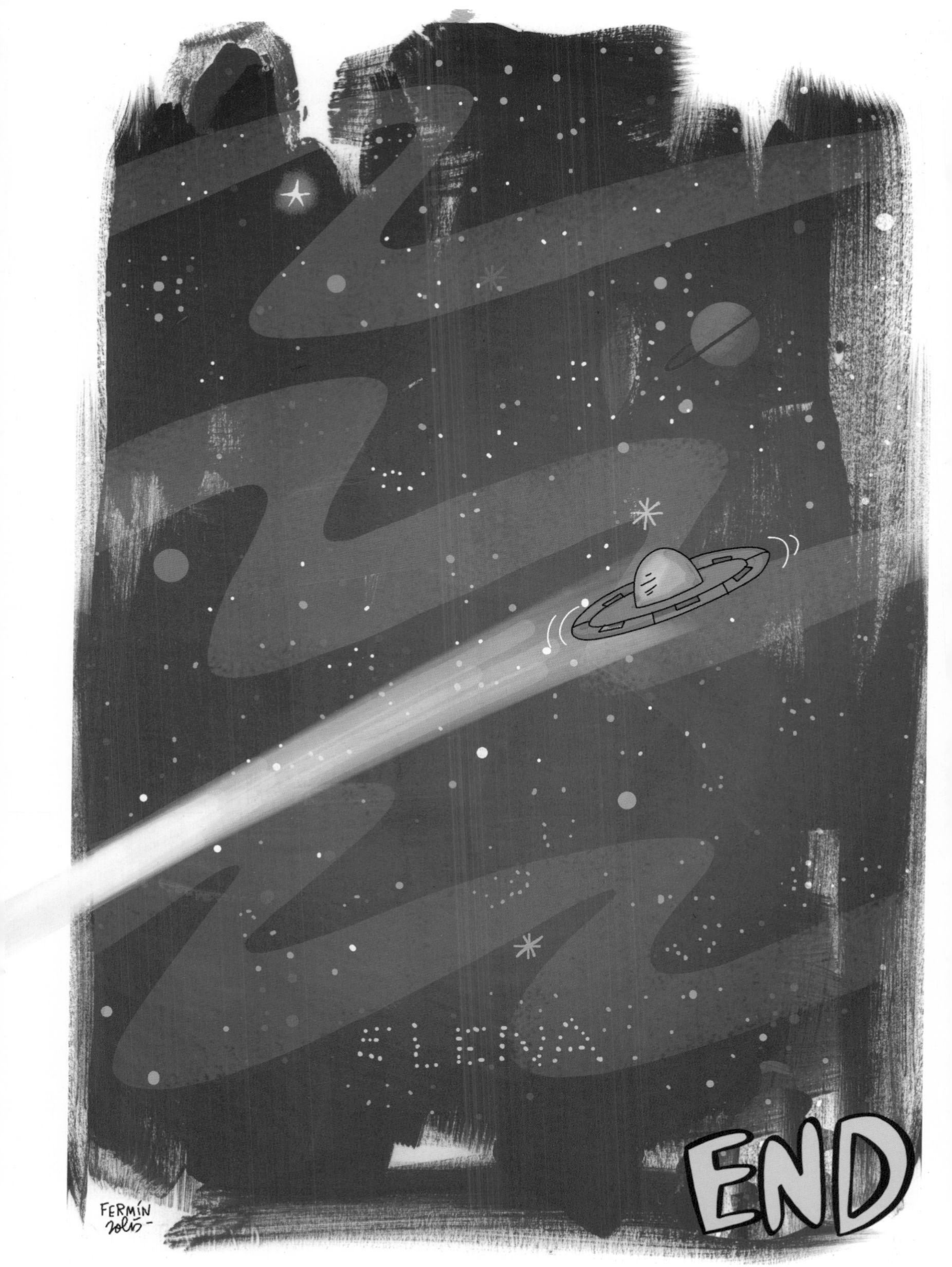
END
FERMÍN
2015-

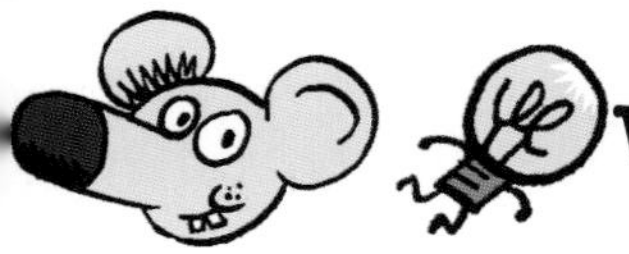

WATCH OUT FOR PAPERCUTZ

Welcome to the funny, first ASTRO MOUSE AND LIGHT BULB graphic novel by Fermín Solís from Papercutz, that modern-day Rat Pack dedicated to publishing great graphic novels for all ages! I'm Jim Salicrup, the Earth-bound Editor-in-Chief and Space Force reject here to pontificate and possibly promote a plethora of Papercutz projects… Up until the publication of this ASTRO MOUSE AND LIGHT BULB graphic novel, it could be argued that Papercutz published so many graphic novels featuring felines we may as well change our name to Paper*catz*. Not only did we at one point publish GARFIELD, but we're currently publishing…

BRINA THE CAT—Brina's a big city cat that can't ever seem to stay at home. If she's not running wild in the countryside exploring the Great Outdoors she's outside of her family's apartment confronting a gang of angry rats on the City's mean streets. BRINA THE CAT author Giorgio Salati "tells an endearing tale…" according to *Publishers Weekly*, while *Kirkus Reviews* opines that artist Christian "Cornia's bright, expressive, animation-inspired art… is the main attraction of this series."

CHLOE & CARTOON—This spin-off series from the popular Charmz series CHLOE by writer Greg Tessier and artist Amandine, tells the tale of how a younger Chloe first met het pet cat Cartoon. The series features actual helpful information on the care and raising of a pet cat along with the same kind of fun stories that's made CHLOE such a hit.

CAT & CAT—The adventures of Catherine, better known to us as just "Cat," and her cat, Sushi, by writers Christophe Cazenove and Hervé Richez and artist Yrgane Ramon. In this series we get to witness the comic escapades of how Cat and her dad first adjusted to having Sushi join their family The fun continues as Cat's dad falls in love with a woman, who is a single mom with a son, and suddenly Cat and Sushi are now in a new blended family.

We could go on and on, mentioning such comical cats as Hubble — the unofficial mascot of THE GEEKY F@B 5, Azrael—Gargamel's pet and sole companion from THE SMURFS TALES, Hot Dog—Lola's pet cat (yes, Hot Dog is a cat!) from LOLA'S SUPER CLUB; Shahruk—Parvati's pet kitten/tiger from the super-hero series THE MYTHICS, and more, but we think you get the idea.

But never let it be said that Papercutz doesn't offer equal time to mice. While we're no longer publishing X-MICKEY (supernatural tales starring Mickey Mouse), MINNIE & DAISY, and THEA STILTON (which featured a group of five female mice who wanted to be reporters like their hero Thea Stilton), we are still publishing GERONIMO STILTON REPORTER (which not only features Geronimo, but his sister Thea Stilton too.), GERONIMO STILTON 3 IN 1 (collecting 3 original GERONIMO STILTON graphic novels in one new paperback edition), and now ASTRO MOUSE AND LIGHT BULB. The mice are *cat*ching up, you might say.

But when it comes to publishing graphic novels featuring sentient light bulbs and caca, we're outpacing all of our competitors! In fact, coming soon is ASTRO MOUSE AND LIGHT BULB #2 "Vs. The Troublesome 4," don't miss it! We hear a certain crooked chicken may be returning as well.

Thanks,
JIM

STAY IN TOUCH!

EMAIL: salicrup@papercutz.com
WEB: papercutz.com
TWITTER: @papercutzgn
INSTAGRAM: @papercutzgn
FACEBOOK: PAPERCUTZGRAPHICNOVELS
FAN MAIL: Papercutz, 160 Broadway, Suite 700, East Wing New York, NY 10038

GO TO PAPERCUTZ.COM AND SIGN UP FOR THE FREE PAPERCUTZ E-NEWSLETTER!

MORE GREAT GRAPHIC NOVEL SERIES AVAILABLE FROM PAPERCUTZ

THE SMURFS TALES

THE ONLY LIVING GIRL

THE ONLY LIVING BOY

THE SISTERS

CAT & CAT

LOLA'S SUPER CLUB

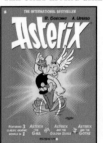
ASTERIX

GERONIMO STILTON REPORTER

DINOSAUR EXPLORERS

GEEKY FAB 5

FUZZY BASEBALL

THE MYTHICS

THE RED SHOES

THE LITTLE MERMAID

BLUEBEARD

GILLBERT

THE LOUD HOUSE

MELOWY

ATTACK OF THE STUFF

GUMBY

PAPERCUTZ™
papercutz.com
Also available as ebooks wherever ebooks are sold.

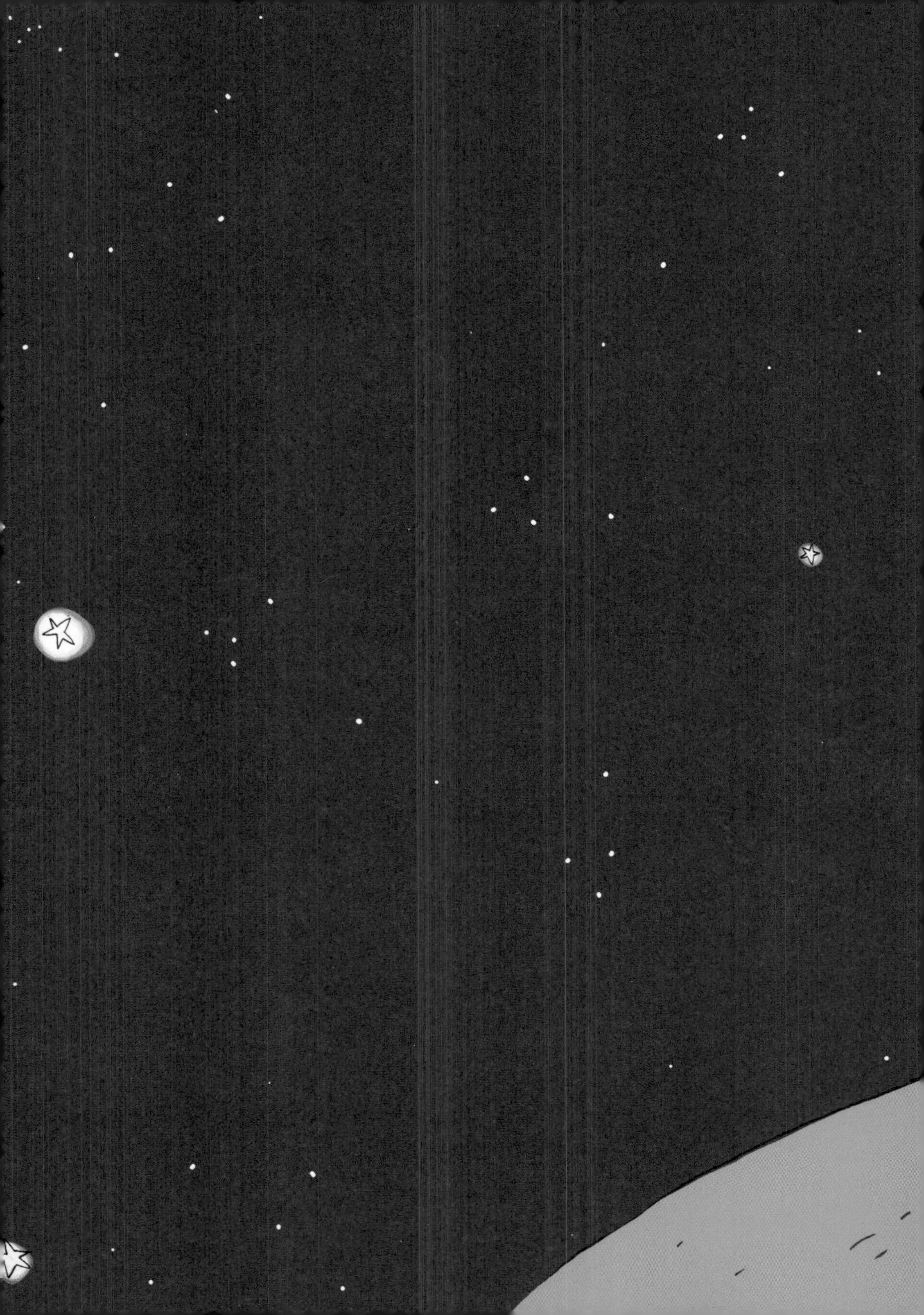